Trinity: Sol 3

Trinity: Sol 3

Andy Wilkinson

The Book Guild

First published in Great Britain in 2025 by
The Book Guild Ltd
Unit E2 Airfield Business Park,
Harrison Road, Market Harborough,
Leicestershire. LE16 7UL
Tel: 0116 2792299
www.bookguild.co.uk
Email: info@bookguild.co.uk
X: @bookguild

Typeset in 10.5pt Adobe Garamond Pro

Printed and bound by CPI Group (UK) Ltd, Croydon, CR0 4YY

ISBN 978 1835741 030

British Library Cataloguing in Publication Data.
A catalogue record for this book is available from the British Library.

MIX
Paper | Supporting responsible forestry
FSC® C013604

I dedicate this book to our family's companion, friend and protector, our beloved Labrador, Buster.

Chapter One

From space, the Earth looks quiet – for a change – recognised by those with interest as a very rare meteorological day in an otherwise chaotic cycle of what scientists have been calling 'global warming' events – events which have violently plagued the planet for the past two decades, without cessation.

Emerging from the darkness of space, a satellite the size of a school bus suddenly adds an edged foreground to the otherwise smooth topography below. At an orbit of 307 nautical miles, the Cold Dark Matter (CDM) Gravity Wave Detector satellite glides silently across the terminator that lies, like a mourning veil, across the Earth, a celestial wall of light segregating the natural world from its dreams and reality. Now it is the turn of those living on the eastern seaboard of the United States to wake up.

The CDM satellite manoeuvres effortlessly and silently. The gold protective cover of the detector reflects sunlight back out into space, the brightness of which momentarily highlights a large, dark blue area of deep water off the Flemish Cap in the north Atlantic Ocean below. As the satellite continues to pitch and yaw into alignment so its solar panels can recharge, small white swirls of cloud can be seen off the west coast of

Africa. These are the remnants of a stalled tropical storm, born in warmer waters a few days earlier.

* * *

Greenbelt, Maryland, is a university town and a commuter suburb to Washington, D.C. and Baltimore, made up primarily of white-collar workers and their families. Large and fast, Greenbelt is situated smack in the middle of four major highways, including the Baltimore-Washington Parkway and the Capital Beltway. It seems the city elders were keen to make Greenbelt an easy place to get to. As planned communities go, its methodical, almost mathematical, layout assured itself as the prime candidate for NASA's first Space Flight Center.

Named after America's rocket pioneer Robert Goddard, it is from here that mission control teams would operate the Burst Alert Telescope (BAT). Goddard is not quite the Hollywood version of mission control. No manned missions are ever monitored from here, as that's the sole prerogative of Mission Control, Houston. The banks of consoles with flight directors, staring unblinkingly at TV monitors, are simply not here at Goddard, which comes as a huge disappointment to the many thousands of visitors the facility gets annually. Goddard is also unique in that missions are often shared by groups of scientists or universities all working on specific individual experiments. However, the satellite now crossing over the Eastern Seaboard of the United States is monitored by only one unique team of scientists. NASA has control over orbital manoeuvres, of course, but the monitoring of Gamma-bursts is really left up to the Cold Dark Matter Team.

Mission control for Project CDM is just a medium-sized room decorated with a few posters, mainly of Jeri Ryan in her *Star Trek* uniform and lots and lots of empty coke cans and pizza boxes. The modest bank of computers in one corner handles the rest.

* * *

"Good morning, Baltimore, this is WBAL 1090 News and Talk Radio – it is 6am on a bright and fresh Monday morning as we cross to Philip Harman in the newsroom for the latest national and international news headlines."

"Good morning. The death toll from the 8.5 magnitude earthquake that struck Northern California three days ago has reached 100,000. The whereabouts of the Governor, Arthur Pendleton, are still unknown, as fears grow that he too is a casualty.

"President Andrews has ordered in the military to co-ordinate rescue operations. Canada, Japan, Mexico, The United Kingdom, and France have all sent rescue teams to help in the relief effort."

Dr. John Kensington jolts awake, with a snort, as his bedside radio alarm clock wakes him. He reaches out with a clenched fist and hits the top of the already cracked clock radio with a sharp downward blow. It hurts. It always does, but the urgency to stop yet another gloomy news report about the Californian quake is an overwhelming necessity, especially today. John feels more irritable than usual this morning, for a couple of reasons, the most immediate of which is that he must get his own coffee this morning.

Slowly edging his warm feet into the cold room air, he turns down the sheets and sits up. Hunched on the edge of the bed, he turns and glances, out of habit, to the other side of the bed. It is empty. He shakes his head in disapproval. Standing, uneasily at first, he moves through the dim light of morning towards the bathroom. He soon stumbles and bangs his toes on an object.

"God damn it!"

Stumbling into the bathroom, he switches on a light and looks down at his toe. Leaning against the door, he examines his foot carefully. All toes seem to be in working order, if just a little red. Placing his foot down gingerly, he looks back into the bedroom. The light has now illuminated the path he created for himself the previous night, between the bathroom and his bed, carefully plotted out so he would not collide with boxes of clothes, books and kids' toys, and a box labelled 'miscellaneous bedroom items', whatever they are, placed on the floor by his wife a few days before.

If that were not enough, he feels irritable this morning because, after five years as a project team leader on CDM, this was his last shift, after which he was out of a job. He still couldn't believe it. Even this prestigious international project, hunting for the missing mass of the universe, had fallen victim to budget cuts.

CDM had saved his marriage. Over the last few years, his astronomy had taken on the mantle of a normal job, working nine to five. No question about it, CDM saved his marriage. A normal working routine meant that his wife, the lovely Beverley, had a husband instead of a stranger writing notes and leaving them on the refrigerator door. They were living two separate lives and were drifting apart.

Every time he thought about his relationship with his wife, Beverley, which was often, he felt uneasy. It was the same feeling he got every time he was about to embark on a long journey. As with most intellectual fears, there was also a funny side; well, in this case, ironic. Not being a big fan of irony, John smiles a bittersweet smile as his mind plays out its cerebral gymnastics while he carefully squeezes that last drop of toothpaste out of the tube.

Like many other astronomy projects that involved pure research, the search for CDM was deemed too insignificant to warrant further funding from the National Space Budget Review Board that year. This is a shame, as the whole purpose of the project was to find the missing ninety-five per cent of the known universe. As John reminded the board in Washington weeks earlier, it would be an important thing to know. He thought wrongly, as it worked out, since the funding was axed days later. The biggest irony of all was that this project, like many others, fell victim to a presidential 'vision for space' – a vision for space? John's smile grew bigger, making his task of brushing his teeth a little easier.

* * *

The drive to the Goddard Space Flight Center from the house takes only ten minutes if the Beltway is free of accidents. Thankfully, it is this morning, and it is a smooth ride in. The car park is already filling up when John pulls his Winchester Grey Honda Accord into a vacant space, alongside a metallic, black GMC Suburban.

Getting out of his small city car, he looks enviously at the Suburban parked next to his. He notices a bumper sticker, blazoned on the rear fender, with the legend: 'Astronomers do it all night long'.

Looking from his small, efficient, clean car with a 'Caution: Child on Board' notice stuck to the rear window, then back to the Suburban with its slick macho appeal, John can't help but shake his head and mumble to himself as he walks to the main entrance of the building.

"*No, Daddy! Think of the environment, Daddy! Besides, I like our little car. Please don't sell Fiona, Daddy, please.*" He snorts. "Kids; who'd have 'em?"

John Kensington walks past reception using his well-rehearsed automatic 'morning' smile and polite acknowledgements. The bitterness at how his team, and many like them, were now being unceremoniously dumped to make way for another presidential folly left a bad taste in his mouth. It wasn't the fault of the staff at Goddard, he knew that, but hey! He wants everyone to know he isn't just another government statistic. He decides on his latest mid-morning fantasy – the one where he finally fires back a classic witty put-down to that sassy, charmless waitress who begrudgingly serves takeout coffee to him at Denny's every morning to the silent cheers of his fellow sufferers – it was about time he let rip!

"Morning, Dr. Kensington."

"Yeah, morning."

His true colours came out as soon as she spoke to him. His wonderful world, where his life was scripted like a Hollywood film, vanished in a puff of smoke. Perhaps today they would notice his newly discovered 'attitude' and somehow it would worm its way back to the Washington budget chiefs and they will, under the pressure of his grouchiness, relent and keep the programme running.

Back in the real world, however, he knows it is time to move on and he needs to breathe fresh air again. Despite his personal problems at home, he really misses his nights of observational astronomy high on a mountainside in Arizona or New Mexico or even Hawaii or New Zealand. Cold pizza never tastes quite as good as when you are eating it on the hood of your jeep, outside an observatory, on some mountainside somewhere, looking up at the stars. It's what real astronomy is all about.

The open-plan office of the CDM team is well lit and there are several of his team already in, clearing their desks. The office is unusually quiet. Missing is the buzz you get when enthusiastic people start talking about their work with other enthusiastic people, the inevitable wisecracking and college dorm humour. It is obvious that today is their last day. The last of the summer wine had been drunk and winter is closing in.

It is all very sad. He knows, as they all do, that when it comes time to say goodbye, the promises of keeping in touch will, predictably, be just a Christmas card for a few years, at most, and the occasional chance meeting at some science conference, in a second-rate hotel in Chicago or Boston.

Surveying the room, Kensington silently watches the subdued handover from the night shift in the mission control office to the first and last of the day watches. A few hugs and handshakes make it official.

"Hey, morning, Obi-Wan. Did the wife leave a map to the kitchen for you?"

"Hey, Karl. Why are you so full of piss and vinegar this morning?"

Karl takes a stapler from a nearby desk and starts to perform the Frank Sinatra hit 'Fly Me To The Moon', swinging his hips too.

"In other words, I start work at JPL on Monday."

A small round of applause comes from the office. Kensington grabs the stapler, puts it back on the desk and looks at Karl, who is beaming back at him.

"Idiot."

"What about you, Kemosabe?"

"What I want to do and what I'm going to—"

"Your wife, right?" Karl interjects.

"Yeah." Trying to be upbeat, Kensington adds, "There is an opening at the Scientific Research Institute and my name has been put forward."

"Look on the bright side! *Star Wars* technology. You can remember back that far, can't you?" Karl smiles a huge smile.

"We'll see. Anything I should know about from the night shift?"

Karl Hunter is young, too damn young to be a section leader of a project like this. But he is smart, despite his youth, and he knows it. He has his whole life before him, and he is going to have a ball with it. Karl is also a damn good astronomer. You hear of natural sportsmen; well, if they ever screened live astronomical observations on ESPN, Karl would be the all-American boy. He had already acquired a reputation as one of the world's leading supernova hunters and was making his name in the hunt for CDM detection. But I guess if you took a spot poll of the rest of the team, they would say his most annoying feature was his good looks. He was damn handsome, not a pretty boy model, but in the Redford or Newman mould. He was the Edwin Hubble of his day, as his old professor at Harvard described him in his reference letter for this post. Karl was the kind of man women loved to be with and men liked to hang out with. In all honesty, Kensington knew how they felt, and it was enough to make the average forty-something Joe Schmuck sick with envy.

I suppose you would also have first to clarify this by saying the majority of the CDM observatory unit were white, single men in their mid-forties and affectionately known round the Goddard centre as 'the vampires'. The uniform of these slightly overweight astronomers was worn with great pride. Black is the favoured colour of their suits, a throwback to 1970s romanticised misconception of what it is to be part of a Gothic sub-culture. Byron, Shelly, and Mary Shelly were the definitive masters of all things dark and malevolent. The customary anchovy pizza breath tops off the Gothic dress sense perfectly. Yes, of course there were exceptions to the rule: Kensington and Anton Medvedenko, CDM's token Russian outstanding scientist, were both married. The rest of the CDM team, including the technicians, male and female, were all single Goths. Girlfriends were thin on the ground and those that were available were Goths too, which didn't help the cause much. Love, in their eyes, being a precursor to tragedy is a hard nut to crack on a first date regardless of who you are. Of all the science fields, astronomy attracted its fair share of the socially challenged and Kensington's team was no exception. Karl was a breath of fresh air to this cliché-riddled bunch.

"Have a look at this baby." Karl hands John a colour photograph of a supernova explosion.

"Hey!" John drops his briefcase and sits on the edge of an empty desk behind him. "A new one? Where did you find this?"

"Yes, sir. It's new alright. Had it confirmed by Barry Sharp in Australia just a minute ago." All the while Karl is telling John of his discovery, he is restless and excited like a small child in a toy shop on Christmas Eve.

"Where?" John adds, without taking his eyes from the image.

"Remember that gravity wave anomaly you and the others found some months ago?"

"Sure, about six months ago, the one in Messier 101, right? Well?"

"Well," Karl is getting even more excited now, "remember you asked me to take a look at it then?"

"And you found this, and you only bring it to me now?" Kensington interrupted.

"No, no; I found nothing, absolutely nothing except what we already knew was there."

"So what is this?" John is slightly irritated now.

"I was calibrating the satellite, using the optical imaging camera; you know, getting it ready for a new target fix. I knew if I pointed it at M101 I would find the usual suspects for my starting point. And *bang*, there it was! A supernova. This, my friend, is M101 last night! Chicken or egg time, John. Is this some sort of echo to your gravity wave anomaly you found six months ago or did M101 just explode?"

John looks up from the photograph. "My God."

John pauses to try and understand his own thoughts a little further, as they flash rapidly across his mind.

"The data we're getting back now is blowing the doors off!" Karl adds to further fluster Kensington.

"Data? What data?" John asks.

"Not sure yet. Anton and that new smart new intern, Rachel, and I are looking over it now. Cool or what?"

Chapter Two

"*Good evening, this is Jules Vernon with the latest from the International Bureau desk: Iran is forging ahead with its nuclear enrichment programme by feeding uranium gas into centrifuge cascades, a report by the United Nations' nuclear watchdog says. Iran had been using a ten-machine cascade and is now testing a twenty-machine version, according to Chief Inspector Mohamed ElBaradei.*

"*He added that, 'In the absence of co-operation from the Iranian Government, he could not say if Iran's aims were purely peaceful.'.*"

The television screen clicks off and goes black. A telephone rings. After the fourth ring, an answerphone picks up.

"*Hi, this is the Kensington family home. We can't take your call now. Leave a message at the tone. Bye.*"

"*John, it's me.*"

It is a woman's voice.

"*We need to talk. I can't go on like this anymore.*" The woman is sobbing. "*You must help me, please, John. If you are home, pick up. John? Call me when you get this.*" The voice falls silent.

The answerphone flashes *10.*

The study is dark except for a single desk lamplight. John Kensington leans forward into the light; he looks exhausted. His eyes are still wide and alert, but the face tells a different story, one of tremendous strain and anguish. Pale and sullen, John strokes his face, which has now accumulated several months' growth of beard. A sudden rush of pain hits his face, as he winces with a toothache. He places a finger inside his mouth to probe the pain. His teeth are stained and unbrushed.

He takes a swig of whiskey from a glass, swills it about his mouth and then swallows hard, with a grimace as the sharp cane liquor bites home. Placing the glass on the desk, he picks up a now very thumbed image of the supernova explosion Karl had handed to him on that last day of normality at the CDM project team headquarters. Kensington gently traces the image with his finger, then carefully pushes the picture to one side. He picks up a second slightly different image of the explosion, an expanding gas ring emanating from a bright core, then a third and a fourth, each showing an even bigger ring of cosmic fire. All four sit on his desk; he layers them one over the other with the least dog-eared image from Karl's deep space images on top.

Taking a clean sheet of paper, he begins to write a letter. There is a sense of urgency and agitation in his manner. The pen flows across the paper with ease, as if what he is writing is well rehearsed. He slowly sits back in his chair, momentarily plunging himself into the darkness that flits around the perimeter of the lamp.

After a moment of silence, John slowly reaches down to a locked desk drawer and opens it with a key that is already in the lock. Putting his hand inside, he pulls out a .38 Smith & Wesson revolver and places it on the desk beside the now finished letter and the images. Picking up the letter, he folds it neatly into an envelope and writes 'RS' on the front.

Taking out his wallet, he empties a huge wad of cash onto the desk, along with his credit cards. He opens another envelope and places the cash and cards inside. He pauses as he addresses the front.

Beverley, forgive me. I love you. He pauses briefly once again before he signs the envelope, *A coward.*

Kensington places the letter at the foot of the desk lamp, next to a picture of his wife and two young daughters. He picks up the photograph and looks at it. He kisses the image of each member of his family.

"Forgive me."

The two envelopes sit side by side on the desk as he picks up the gun. Standing, he switches off the desk lamp and the room plunges into darkness. A glimmer of moonlight frames the patio doors that lead to the garden. John opens the doors and steps out into the cold night air.

A car quietly pulls up along the path that runs by the side of the house. John looks over to where the engine sound is, and a warm smile briefly crosses his face. A lone figure, silhouetted by the moonlight, stands overlooking the garden.

John walks towards his kids' swing and pauses. Taking a deep breath, John looks across at the figure and nods in acknowledgement. Wiping his nose with the sleeve of his right arm, the pistol hangs loosely in his hand. John sits on the swing and slowly rocks back and forth. Looking up into the night sky, he suddenly stops. With a deep inner sigh, John relaxes his posture and gently begins to rock himself on the swing again. Slowly, he raises the revolver to the side of his head and places the barrel against his temple.

"Beverley, I love you."

Closing his eyes, he pulls the trigger. His body falls to the grass like a sack of flour as his legs momentarily catch on the swing before they too fall to the grass.

The swing continues to sway over the length of his body, forwards, then backwards. Suddenly, a gloved hand stops the motion of the swing.

* * *

The light from the flashlight cuts the darkness of the study with its powerful beam. Like a World War II anti-aircraft searchlight, it crosses the room in a pattern, searching for its target. The light stops as it finds John Kensington's desk.

The figure quickly moves to the desk and scans the items on it. Seeing the letters, he picks them both up and puts them inside his coat. His attention now turns to the photographic images on the desk. Picking them up, one at a time, he briefly looks at them all. Pausing momentarily, he tears them in half. One piece falls to the floor, and he slowly bends to pick it up. The flashlight momentarily reflects his image back to him from his highly polished, stylised, patent leather shoes. He puts the pieces into his pocket and leaves through the patio doors, as silently as he came.

* * *

The radio messages, interspersed with static bursts, are a clear sign that the police have arrived. From the outside, Dr. John Kensington's house now looks like a day-old wedding reception. White and blue plastic tape decorates various areas of the house and garden. The local Greenbelt police are here in force. A police car now blocks the small dirt-track road that skirts the Kensington home. The crime forensic examination teams are in full swing as they examine the house and garden, dressed in their now familiar all-in-one, pure white, disposable suits.

Parked just a little way down, near the side garden entrance, is the coroner's black stretch Cadillac. Reporters from both *The Washington Post* and *Baltimore Sun* sip steamy cups of Starbucks' coffee from logo-emblazoned Styrofoam, shuffling their feet to keep warm in the cold morning air.

The local Metro TV news crew arrives like a military

parade, pulling their large trucks, bedecked with aerials and satellite dishes, into a small natural lay-by at the rear of the garden. Like storm troopers, the camera crew leap out of the truck via sliding side doors and immediately start to set up their equipment of lights and cameras. The sole objective of this warlike operation is to capture the moving image of NBC's hottest new television correspondent, Crystal Murphy.

Murphy is a woman on a mission. From the moment she left UCLA, armed with a bachelor's degree in political science, she knew, as did NBC who were now grooming her, that she would one day take over the mantle of lead news anchor from Stone Phillips and reach the ultimate accolade not even presidents obtain: that of the most trusted face in America.

Still in her mid-twenties, naturally blonde and blessed with Hollywood good looks, Murphy is trying hard to look a lot older than she is. The public relation advice from New York was that the face of a nation's trust rests slightly better on the face of one who has at least lived a little first.

Like a royal princess, Murphy calmly slides out of the front passenger seat of the TV truck to be waited on by the modern-day equivalent of a lady-in-waiting – in this case, the unit runner, Sarah. A fresh Danish pastry is handed to Murphy, as is a fresh cup of coffee served in a clean china cup. Murphy acknowledges her fellow news gatherers huddled nearby with a shallow nod of her head aimed in their general direction. It must be said, each of them smiles cordially back, albeit through gritted teeth and silent profanity, as they reflect on how she may have got her first big break in the cut-throat arena of television news reporting.

It is not unusual to find animosity between rivals in the news-gathering circle, especially on a hot 'Top Scientist Found Dead' feeding frenzy news day like today. The fast-food fix that is TV journalism, appeasing the twenty-four-hour society we now live in, and the analytical, crafted prose of writers whose words will be lining birdcages tomorrow have never welcomed each other warmly into their own camps. But, like some forgotten Geneva conventions, an armistice between them is dutifully maintained on such news-gathering occasions.

This transitory truce, however, is quickly broken by the sudden appearance of two men in dark full-length raincoats wheeling an ambulance-style trolley, with a black body bag lying on it, to the rear of the coroner's car. With little ceremony, they all rush to photograph and question the two men. The press pack soon resembles the offensive line of an American football team who have just fumbled on their own five-yard line in the fourth quarter of a championship game. Ignoring the scrum, the two assistant coroners place John Kensington's body into the back of the van and quickly close the doors.

Like deflated dolls, shoulders slumped and with bowed heads, the press corps return to their respective camps to light up more cigarettes and drink yet more tepid coffee.

* * *

The Watergate Hotel, as all political historians know, is still located at 2650 Virginia Ave NW, Washington, D.C. This five-star hotel remains the hub of the movers and shakers in the world of global politics. The infamous Watergate break-ins that brought down President Nixon on 9 August 1974 are now a footnote in academic books on the history of America. Films and documentaries have been made, but they all pale into insignificance in the light of the political schisms that now exist in modern-day America. What has not changed over almost five decades in the heart of Washington, however, is the stalwart of political intrigue which plays host to the puppet masters of the world. It is The Watergate Hotel.

The lobby of the Watergate Hotel is as luxurious as any five-star hotel you may have had the pleasure to visit, except for one thing. Sprinkled about the lobby, like guests at a funeral service convention, are men, tall men. They are all dressed the same way: in dark black suits, black ties, black socks and shoes; sporting crew-cut hairstyles, ear radio pieces, microphones in their left hands; and with bulging left pockets in their suit jackets. This is Fortress Watergate, a sight which does not phase the reception staff in the slightest, as it is a common occurrence when the hotel is hosting a special meeting. Today is no exception. Access to the penthouse conference room is heavily guarded by the mortician brigade. The room is, however, now ready for the meeting to begin.

The room is in darkness to hinder any rogue photographer with a telephoto lens across the street in another building. Only shadows can be seen by a single circular fluorescent light emanating from the ceiling.

"Thank you for all coming so promptly. We do have an issue which is why you, the Nova Collective, have been assembled."

It is an elderly man who speaks, bringing the individuals to order. No introduction by name, just a sense of calmness, a clarity of voice, unrushed, and mature in nature. Had you been there, you would immediately envision a demeanour of authority from his voice alone. Chairs are heard shuffling as the assembly seat themselves. The first man speaks again.

"We all know that the higher echelons of the science community are small. Everyone knows everyone else, what projects they are working on and with whom. The internet, with its instantaneous communication, is the blood that circulates through the veins of this science community. Knowledge passes freely between them. Unfortunately, the informational blood flow has developed a haemorrhage."

A low mumbling is heard.

"You are therefore called," the gravitas of the first speaker resonates in the conference room, "to vote on our next action."

There is a pause. Then once again his voice rumbles.

"The National Security Agency will, inevitably, as is its function, assign an agent to investigate this haemorrhage. This agent must complete their task without any interference from an outside source. This investigation must, therefore, be a DOA case. Dead On Arrival at the desk of the NSA who instigated it. No further investigation. File closed."

"How can we be sure of that outcome?" This time a new voice is heard, for the first time. A Russian voice: good English, yet the deep unforgiving tones of a Muscovite can clearly be heard underlying it. The Russian expands his thoughts: "We can assign an agent who is perhaps not the best at their job. An undisciplined mandarin, someone who is easy to manipulate and who will follow the leads we lay down for them."

"Do we know of such an agent?" the first speaker asks.

"I think I do." A woman is in the room. Her voice, although soft, has a resonance that is clearly understood. "I have a list of agents with me. At the bottom of the list is the man we should assign, or at least think about."

"And what is this agent's name?"

"Paul Mitchell. Mitchell has been sent to our listening station in Greenland as a punishment for insubordination, among other things."

"Other things?" Another new voice, rich and sonorous, joins in the conversation.

"Yes, a list of offences, such as: not following orders, being a soft touch for his targets on apprehension, an easy happy-go-lucky attitude to most NSA assignments. This is a man I would suggest fits our agenda."

The first speaker coughs gently. "We shall now vote. The Nova Collective must remain anonymous. Paul Mitchell must fail in his investigation. Your votes, please, on assigning Paul Mitchell to the CDM investigation. I will go around the table."

Everyone responded affirmatively.

"Excellent. Akin to the Lord's disciples in the bible, we twelve members of the Nova Collective have decided that Agent Paul Mitchell is our man."

* * *

Paul Mitchell is tired. He looks down at his old-fashioned pocket watch, a beautiful piece of workmanship inherited from his grandfather, that is sitting on a fold-down tray in front of him.

"Christ," he silently mouths. Was it only two hours ago that he was in his quarters asleep? Now he is being buffeted about in a cold C-130 transport plane heading to Andrews Air Force Base in Washington, D.C.

His brain has not yet caught up with his nocturnal activity of catching airplanes in the middle of the night. Silently, his mind rants: *Andrews. Now, that's the home of Air Force One. Now, why couldn't they have sent that to Greenland to pick me up?* Mitchell's mind muses further as he pockets his watch, stows the pull-down tray in front of him and drags the coarse hair blanket up further across his chest. *Instead of this flying truck. Come on, Paul, get a little sleep. It will make the time pass more quickly.* His mind has finally evaluated the situation and decides on the best course of action, which is to shut down for a while.

"This is Captain Bains on the flight deck."

Mitchell's eyes spring open.

"Mr. Mitchell. I thought you would like to know that the flight time to Andrews is six hours, twenty minutes; a bit of head wind is slowing us down tonight. Try and get some sleep." The speaker crackles with static then falls silent.

"Aye, aye, Captain," Mitchell whispers back, "aye, aye."

Six hours of cold, turbulent flying with no in-flight service or movie; he shivers at the thought – *marvellous.* Taking the only luxury afforded him on the flight – plastic earphones – he plugs them in and listens to the single station on offer – the BBC World Service.

"*On today's programme, we will be looking at the worrying downtrend in the number of people attending church, not only with Christian worship, but in synagogues and temples across the world. Joining me in the studio to discuss this is Rabbi…*"

"Perhaps I'll forgo the in-flight entertainment," Mitchell says to himself, as he pulls the plug on the Beeb and settles back into the struggle that is sleep.

* * *

The drive into Greenbelt from Andrews is straightforward and Mitchell is grateful for that, as the heater in his motor pool-assigned car seems capable of only pumping out cold air. Mitchell thinks it was either busted or fixed that way by a motor pool mechanic as a favour to some officer based in a Baghdad suburb, and he simply forgot to switch it back when it was shipped back. Adapt and survive, as they say.

Go, marines! Oorah!

Now switched off, the condensation from his body heat – whatever there was left of it, anyway – mixing with the cold air makes all the interior windows mist over. The right sleeve of his coat is wet with wiping the window screen clear on the forty or so mile journey he has just taken. The sight of a police car blocking his path further up the dirty track is a welcoming one. He has arrived.

One of two policemen approach as Mitchell lowers the driver's window. It is difficult not to notice the swaggering authority county policemen get when a 'real' crime occurs on their turf. 'I'm a real policeman today; you can shove your traffic citations up your ass today, bud, I'm a cop!' Knowing words poised on every lip but spoken in gesture only.

"Sorry, sir, this area is restricted to official police personnel only." He smiles. "Are you press? You'll find your buddies a bit further down the road. The chief will give you guys a statement later when he's ready." A raised hand accompanied the words, like John Wayne waving a path to your next destination.

In a way, deep down perhaps, Mitchell really didn't like doing what he was about to do. After all, every dog has its day. Mitchell produces his identification badge.

The police officer studies the badge insolently, reading the identification out loud.

"What is this then? Mitchell, Paul." He pauses, trying hard not to let his disappointment show as he continues to read. "NSA – National Security Agency."

Mitchell was the one person he couldn't bully today.

"Er, okay, Mr. Mitchell. The chief is in the house. You can go on up."

"Thanks." Mitchell keeps his broad smile hidden deep within his face.

Mitchell gets out of his car and closes the door. The second officer, taking his cue from his colleague, lifts the cordon tape and lets Mitchell pass under.

The walkie-talkie belt clip snaps shut as the disappointed police officer draws the transmitter up to his mouth in a smooth, practised motion.

"Chief, Paul Mitchell of the NSA is on his way up to see you now."

"Oh, fucking great!" is the static-polluted reply.

* * *

As Mitchell enters the garden, he can see the route the deceased had taken to the swing. The initial report he read on the flight to Washington was about just that. A body was found, in a garden, beneath a child's swing.

The early morning dew had lain heavy on the grass this morning and the footprints could be easily seen. Following the footprints with his eyes, Mitchell can see a large, flattened area of grass just below the child's swing. The succinct report was proved to be correct.

Walking slowly towards the swing, making sure to skirt any evidence that might still be found, Mitchell looks at the area of the impression. Not a chalk outline as such, but still, a clearly defined torso with legs can be made out. A red stain on the grass marked where Kensington's head had fallen, blood seeping from a head wound into the lawn, staining it red. Mitchell suddenly thinks of an old rhyme his mother used to say when getting dressed for an evening soiree with his father at his lodge – 'red and green should never be seen'. It always made him smile but looking at the bloodstain on the lush green grass, his mother had never been more right.

There is something else that strikes him as odd. The footprints of the scene of the crime team can be distinguished from Kensington's because the soles of their boots are smooth, but there are two distinct patterns left in the morning dew. One set leads back up to the house. Kensington was not alone.

The study is a hive of activity when Mitchell steps in from the garden. Police officers and members of the county forensic examiner's office are busy dusting for prints and making long memos in old notebooks.

"You Mitchell?"

His accent is from the Deep South, Alabama perhaps. His tone is slow, purposeful and to the point. It makes him stand out, even more than his appearance does. His career has sculpted his body over the years. He is overweight – too much junk food on stakeouts – five o'clock shadow in the morning means he shaved last night, badly co-ordinated dress sense means he's no longer married: a typical career policeman. He straightens his tie and brushes cigarette ash from his jacket to the dismay of the forensic examiner standing nearby.

Mitchell produces his ID. This time, it is ignored by the officer.

"I'm Captain Leo Franklin, Greenbelt PD. Pleased to meet you." Franklin extends his hand. Mitchell shakes it.

"Special Agent Paul Mitchell, NSA."

The fussing of the forensic examiner momentarily distracts Mitchell.

"We knew that Kensington worked at Goddard, but I didn't think he would warrant such a high level of interest from Washington—"

"Greenland," Mitchell interjected.

"Greenland?" Franklin was taken aback.

"Yes, sir, my office is in Greenland."

"Jesus Christ, they couldn't find anyone nearer?" Franklin laughs.

"Tell me about it." Mitchell smiles as he moves past Franklin further into the room.

Franklin shrugs and moves with Mitchell into the room. "No point fighting the bureaucrats at City Hall, I guess."

"John Kensington – anything on him?" Mitchell looks at the desk.

Franklin walks over towards a window in the study and looks out to the garden. "Nope, never had a brush with the law except the usual traffic violations. Paid the fine promptly too. Typical professor type; you get a lot of them round here." Franklin taps a pain of glass in the French doors with a finger knuckle. "Found the body under the garden swing. His head had a hole the size of a shot glass in it."

Mitchell walks over, stands by Franklin, and looks at the wood surround of the French doors.

"Any sign of a forced entry into the house?" The wood feels smooth under his fingers, but he needs to ask the question, nonetheless.

"None that we could find. The side door leading into the garden was open. We've dusted for prints, but only found one set so far and my guess is they're his."

"You find that odd?" Mitchell looks back into the room. "I mean, this looks like a family house, not your typical bachelor pad, and only one set of prints."

"We understand his wife and family moved out some months ago, again not an unusual occurrence about here. I mean, they may study the light fantastic, but they sure don't live it – know what I mean?" Franklin laughs out loud, while Mitchell smiles politely. Franklin controls his indulgence and continues, "And we thought that too. His housemaid was the last to see him alive, cleans for him on a regular basis – hence the single set of prints."

Mitchell reaches into his pocket and takes out a clear plastic spray bottle.

"Any objections if, after your forensic team have finished, I have a look for prints?"

Franklin looks at the spray bottle.

"Sure, no problem. What's that you've got there?"

Mitchell holds the bottle out for Franklin. Franklin takes it eagerly and shakes it. A clear liquid is inside.

"This is new. In fact, we and the FBI are the only agencies to have it. For testing, but so far it is leaps and bounds over the toxic dusting of finger printing."

"Oh yeah? What is it."

"It is a British university discovery. They use the protein from jellyfish in this neutral solution to spray on items that may have fingerprints. No cross contamination at all and it shows you, the examiner, if there are fingerprints present."

Mitchell walks back to the French windows and touches them.

"Here, look, spray a little here and see for yourself."

Franklin does and immediately Mitchell's handprint shows up clearly.

"Heavens to Betsy, that is incredible. When do we get this?"

"That information is way above my pay grade. I am still waiting for my Apollo moon mission jetpack!"

Franklin hands back the bottle, laughing, nodding and shrugging all at the same time.

Mitchell asks, "So what are you going to call it, Captain?"

Franklin stands tall, proud to be seen as the one still calling the shots. He tucks his shirt back inside the front of his pants.

"A single gunshot wound to the head at point blank range, I think we can notch this one up as a suicide."

Franklin moves to sit in a high-backed leather-bound reading chair in the corner of the study. Dropping his weight into the chair, he sighs, as the buttons on his shirt begin to strain with the extra force now exerted on them.

"We get them from time to time here too. Especially among the eggheads we've got living here. They blow a gasket at the office and blow their brains out at home. Seen it all before."

Mitchell nods. "Did he leave a note?"

"A note?" Franklin is caught off guard.

"Yes, a note. People who commit suicide usually leave a note. Did any of your people find one?"

"No, not that I have been told about anyway." The once

comfortable chair Franklin is sitting in seems to have become hot as he shifts his weight again.

"Suicides don't normally hide them," Mitchell adds. "Get your people to search again, just in case."

Franklin stands.

"I'm sure we'd have found one, but no problem." Turning, Franklin beckons to one of his deputies.

"Yes, Captain?"

Franklin's tone is less than supportive as his unsuspecting and bewildered subordinate takes on the mantle of whipping boy.

Franklin is obviously annoyed with himself more than his deputy as Mitchell respectfully retreats to examine Kensington's desk.

"Who found the body?" Mitchell breaks the wrath of command being laid down.

"His housemaid. Like I said, we're questioning her now."

Franklin dismisses his deputy with a wave of his hand, as if swatting an invisible fly.

"We've also asked her to look around the house and she's certain nothing's been stolen. Don't know how reliable that is; she's shaken up."

"Any idea what time the incident occurred?" Mitchell takes off his jacket and places it over the back of the desk chair.

Franklin stands in front of the desk, now with his hands on his hips and his stomach temporarily highlighted by the absence of his suit jacket.

"The body was found at seven-thirty this morning. The medical examiner put the time of death at about midnight."

"What about the neighbours – anyone hear the gun shot?"

"No, it's pretty isolated here."

Mitchell quickly looks back out of the study window at the child's swing. Franklin is curious what else he has missed.

"Okay. That's helpful, Captain, thanks. I'll just nose about here if that's okay with you?"

"Sure, go ahead." Franklin turns to leave. A few steps further on, he suddenly stops. "Mr. Mitchell, I know you people at the NSA like to keep your secrets, but don't keep anything away from me that's relevant to my investigation. NSA or not, this is still my party – okay?"

Mitchell, for the first time that day, finds he is now in a two-way conversation. Up until then he was a one-man squawk box, routine questions and verbal identification replies was all he had uttered since leaving Greenland. The captain had caught Mitchell off guard and, even while he was replying, he knew it sounded more earnest than was necessary.

"Captain, if I find anything, rest assured I'll call you immediately."

A sceptical look flashes across Franklin's face that Mitchell recognises was entirely his fault.

With a contrite look, Mitchell watches the captain leave the study. The chief sweeps his arms and claps loudly, indicating to his men that it is time to leave. The captain now has the air of a man who had just been hoodwinked, knew it and can't do a damn thing about it. But Mitchell could do nothing about it now, either.

* * *

Kensington's desk is tidy. A greyish-white powder from the earlier forensic tests has settled, like day-old icing on a sponge cake. A large, green-coloured desk protector, edged with a gold fleur-de-lis motif, sits, centrally, on the desk.

Mitchell eases himself into the desk chair and studies the items on the desk one by one: a lamp, a pen, an answerphone machine with no tape cassette inside. *Forensics must have it*, he concludes. Mitchell takes his clear bottle of spray and presses the top button a few times. A fine mist envelopes the desk, over the white powder.

Just one set of prints, near the desk protector only.

Kensington's.

Sitting back, Mitchell casually looks around the study. It is neat and orderly. *Odd*, he thinks. All the scientists he had ever known, though admittedly they were mainly computer nerds that the NSA seemed to attract like wasps to jam, were the messiest, most disorganised bunch of people he had ever come across.

A habit Mitchell had acquired since working for the NSA, while he was thinking, was for his hands to unconsciously do a tactile investigation of the surface in front of him. From years of waiting for computer deciphers to decode millions of bits of information, he surmised, whenever he caught himself doing it. However, this time his sensitive fingers catch a distinctive indentation. This discovery snaps him back into focus. Mitchell switches on the desk lamp and immediately tips the light to illuminate the desk. Lowering his face so that his cheek brushes the surface, he traces the indentations once again with his fingers. There is something here.

Sitting up slightly, he finds a scrap of paper and takes a pencil from his pocket. Placing the paper over the indentations, he gently shades over it with his pencil. Slowly, words begin to emerge amongst the recent doodles, and holding the finished work up to the light, he can read:

R
Can't tinue. o much pr es knows I need to tal . I
you'll understand.
I'll be ing for you the othersi Be areful e may
after all us John

It wasn't much. But it was a start.

Chapter Three

Captain Franklin hits the brakes late and the car skids to a halt on the wet tarmac of Reagan Airport. Mitchell is held tightly by his seatbelt as Franklin curses the ABS on the squad car.

"Yeah, sorry about that." It was a poor apology. "These lousy anti-skid brakes only make you skid more. If I could find the fucking off-switch, I'd turn the damn things off. I swear to God, I would!" Franklin hits the dashboard with his fist.

"I do appreciate the ride, Chief," Mitchell says with as much confidence as he could muster.

"Here." Franklin reaches behind himself to the back seat. He grabs a thin report in a document sleeve and hands it to Mitchell.

"The autopsy revealed nothing other than I expected. It was a .38 special, point blank. Cause of death: massive blood loss due to severe head trauma to the right temporal lobe."

"In other words," Mitchell summarises.

"Suicide," they say simultaneously. Both smile.

Franklin drives the car faster than Mitchell likes through the open wire-fence gates that lead to the helipad station of the airport. Franklin brakes on arrival, testing the seatbelt anchors once again.

"The helicopter will take you directly to NSA HQ in Washington, Mr. Mitchell. Have a good flight."

Franklin offers Mitchell his hand.

"Thanks. And again, thanks for the ride." Mitchell shakes his hand.

Getting out of the car, Mitchell battles his overcoat with the downwash of the rotor blades. Franklin watches him go, suspecting it won't be the last time he will have dealings with NSA Agent Paul Mitchell.

* * *

The National Security Agency building in Washington, D.C. is the flagship building of the agency. Elegant yet intimidating, it is the public face of the NSA and home to the Washington mandarins who secure huge chunks of the nation's tax dollars to operate it. The building was never designed to be the ears and eyes of the nation, just the home to some of the best brains in America.

It has been over three years since he was last here. The marble floor of the lobby is still grey and uninviting, and, since 9/11, the entrance has taken on the look of a crime scene, with uniformed officers and barriers blocking entrances and exits.

Mitchell walks with purpose to the security check-in desk and identifies himself. A simple nod of the officer's head allows the turnstile gate to rotate and open and, at the same time, signals the burly, machine gun-armed officer guarding it to move to one side and let him pass.

At the elevators, Mitchell hits the up button and waits. The lift is empty, and Mitchell takes a solo ride up to the seventh floor. The doors open silently, unlike all the futuristic TV shows he watches on dull evenings at home where all the doors seem to open with a hissing sound. Mitchell steps out. Directly in front of him is yet another reception area and security check point. However, this time the customary logo of the NSA Investigations Bureau hangs on the wall behind the familiar face of Ms. Henshaw, the Washington departmental receptionist who has been with the agency, it seems, forever.

Ms. Henshaw knows everyone by sight. No one can get past her without her knowing them.

"Paul Mitchell." He offers his ID for inspection.

"Good to see you back, Mr. Mitchell." Ms. Henshaw is a marvel. "Miss Sands is expecting you." She hands Mitchell back his ID.

At that moment, Joanna Sands, Mitchell's boss and head of the Investigations Bureau, appears from an office suite further down the corridor. She is showing someone out, directing them to Henshaw at reception. She sees Mitchell standing by Henshaw's desk.

Sands is tall, athletic, with shoulder length, dark hazel-coloured hair. However, your first impressions, if you fall into that trap, would be wrong if you thought Sands had an active social and love life. 'You can never judge a book by its cover' is such an accurate attitude to have, as Mitchell discovered. A first look did deceive, to his cost, on their first meeting some years previously.

You see, Joanna Sands is what the NSA classifies as a genius; not just a very smart woman being recruited directly from an Ivy League educational establishment, but also a pure polymath. She is an exceptional, all-round genius. Okay, the word Genius is used far too frequently these days. It dilutes the standard. How many times do you hear sports commentators cry out 'the boy's a genius' when a million-dollar quarterback throws a ball to someone without falling over their own feet in the process? No, the title 'genius' should have a reserved notice attached in a footnote: 'only to be used in association with the likes of Einstein, Hawking, Newton and, yes, Sands'.

Even Sands, in her own indomitable eclectic fashion, is a genius of equal rank. She has been known to solve the London *Times* cryptic crossword as if she were making a grocery list, while holding a four-way telephone conference with fellow code breakers trying to solve a problem.

Two bucks would give you ten that she was the one who found a solution to the problem first. And that's her problem. She doesn't do small talk well and has a low threshold of boredom. That is why Sands can't do the role-play games of courtship well: she is far too logical and rational, and love is anything but logical or rational. Sands has yet to find anyone who is her mental equal – who isn't old enough to be her grandfather, that is. Being a genius is a very lonely profession, perhaps a curse, Mitchell concluded.

"Paul, good to see you. Keeping warm enough in Greenland?" Sands is already walking back into her office as she speaks.

"Just about." Mitchell increases his step to keep up.

"Worked out yet which director of operations you pissed off to get that posting?" Sands is already sorting papers on her desk when Mitchell arrives at her doorway.

"I thought it was you." Mitchell smiles, looking for a response in her face.

"Hell no! The list of senior agents and directors you've pissed off over the years looks like an entry in a Sears catalogue."

Mitchell is pleased with his fumbled attempt at a humorous remark. The last one fell flat on their first casual date, years ago, and now it seems no longer to be an issue.

"How did it go in Greenbelt?" Sands points to an empty chair in front of her desk that Mitchell throws his coat over. He sits in the empty one beside it.

"Fine, I guess. The local constabulary were a little put out that I was even there, and it wasn't long before I started getting the 'grassy knoll' conspiracy look."

Sands snorts a laugh, a cute gesture by her standards.

"Suicide is what they're calling it in Greenbelt, despite the absence of a suicide note. Is there anything in Kensington's death that should concern us?"

"Well, whatever happened, there is a strong possibility that someone cleaned-up after the event and made damn sure to cover their tracks."

Sands, for the first time in this conversation, stops doing half a dozen things at once and looks directly at Mitchell.

"What makes you think that?"

"Well, I found indications that there was a suicide note. I grant you, he could have posted it before he killed himself but that's not the usual MO. I have people looking into it. I did manage to get a stencil of what I think is part of it, however." Mitchell produces a neatly folded piece of paper from his suit jacket pocket.

"Where did you get this from?" Sands enquires, as she is handed the note.

"From the impressions left on the desk protector. Signed, apparently, by Dr. Kensington himself."

"Wow!" Sands reads the note. "What a find. Did you know that most suicide notes are typed these days or left on a computer's open page?"

"I didn't. You learn something new every day." Paul looks around the office for a coffee pot. He sees one and stands to pour himself a cup, since he hasn't been offered any. "May I?"

"Oh, sure. Sorry, bad manners."

Mitchell pours himself a cup of hot coffee.

"Jo, I think I should keep my nose in this for a bit longer. Otherwise, it seems a waste of taxpayers' money to fly me all the way here from my frozen home sweet home just to agree with Greenbelt PD."

"I agree. What's your next step?"

"I'm sending the stencil down to the calligraphy department for examination and verification, to see if it really is John Kensington's handwriting."

Sands nods in agreement.

"I'll give it to Cameron too. He's the best analyst we've got here. Let's see what he can make of it," Mitchell adds.

"Assuming Kensington did write the note," Sands hands the note back to Mitchell, "it still doesn't answer the question of who took it – if someone did – or why."

Sands seats herself behind her desk and opens a file. As she reads, she thinks out loud.

"The Scientific Research Institute was set up years ago to utilise the technology and materials originally developed for the Strategic Defence Initiative programme. Why would he resign from that?"

Sands looks up from the report as Mitchell takes his seat again, coffee in hand.

"Another puzzle, here. Why, with all this SDI technology and funding floating about in the system, all unused and spoken for, did he jump ship? It says here he had been made head of the CDM project, utilising some of that tech and funds. The CDM project was getting results, so it says in here, and then *bang*. He kills himself. Why? He resigned from the Scientific Research Institute, the umbrella company of CDM project, before all this. Heavens, why?"

Mitchell leans forward to try and read the document Sands is looking at.

"Yes, two weeks ago," he chips in.

Sands looks up. Her eyes are a giveaway. Her brain had moved up a gear, as a mystery beckoned that sought a solution.

Mitchell looks at Sands with a comforting realisation. These mysteries are the reason she breathes.

* * *

Mitchell stands beside the seated Joanna Sands and reads the document over her shoulder.

"Does it give a reason for his resignation?"

Sands licks the tip of her thumb and turns a page over.

"Yes, here it is – 'disaffection with the project'." She pulls a letter from the file and hands it to Mitchell to read. "This is the original resignation letter."

Mitchell scans the letter quickly. "Fairly rambling; on the lines of, 'What the hell is the point of doing all this?' Strange way to bow out of a successful career and project." Mitchell hands the letter back to Sands for her to replace in the file. "Is there any evidence he was a spook for the other side?" Mitchell moves to take his seat again.

"None. He went through the usual security checks before he was employed at the SRI. He seemed to be a good choice according to the assessment panel that interviewed him. But as history tells us, it wouldn't be the first time a spy had infiltrated our system."

"LeRoy Nicholson back in 2013. I remember. No one suspected him except you, Jo."

Sands blushes. She looks up from her desk at Mitchell.

"Nicholson was CIA who turned on his own. Kensington worked at the SRI, a toothless bird. Who would gain by Kensington's death?"

"There is a lot of sensitive and dangerous technology

developed through that organisation. Kensington had a comprehensive knowledge of all of it," Mitchell interjects into the conversation, turning the proverbial gas up to see if the milk will boil over.

Sands looks to the coffee jug on the side table. "More coffee?"

"Sure, thanks."

Sands takes Mitchell's mug as she moves from behind her desk and pours two cups. She offers one to Mitchell.

The coffee is hot; however, nothing like the fine richness of Mitchell's first cup. Instead, it has been replaced with a hot liquid, bland, with a flatness of taste, like a liquid dusty powder. Stewed is the common adjective used to describe this cup of coffee. A familiar taste found in offices the world over.

Mitchell winces.

Sands sits on the edge of her desk facing Mitchell. In normal circumstances, the distance between them now would be considered close, even intimate. She smelt good – apple blossom. The way she looks and acts could have been interpreted as flirtatious, but Mitchell knows better. He has enough problems. Professionally, he cages his libido, a skill he learnt through a series of undercover operative training sessions with the CIA. But then again – what if?

"We have to be certain that there has been no breach of national security in this, Paul."

Mitchell is abruptly made to refocus on the task at hand.

"Without question. Okay, I'll need access to all the relevant files he was working on. I don't know if my security clearance will cover that?"

"It will by the time you finish your coffee." Sands moves back behind her desk and picks up the phone. "Ms. Henshaw, would you come in here for a moment please?"

Sands carefully replaces the phone back on its cradle.

Mitchell continues, "I'll go and introduce myself to his

colleagues. We need to find out what Kensington's mental state was prior to two weeks ago."

"Good, I'll arrange for you to meet with Dr. Henry Eidelman. He took over from Kensington at the institute. Also, find out if there are any foreign agencies operating over here that could be involved. I'd like this thing cleared up as quickly as possible, Paul, one way or another."

Mitchell stands and starts to put his coat on.

"I'll try digging more into his past, find out if he had any personal enemies that would want him dead."

Mitchell walks to the door and finds Ms. Henshaw waiting there.

Sands raises her voice, only a little, but it is clear, and her voice resonates within the room.

"Get back to me as soon as you can on this one. You know how I hate unsolved puzzles."

* * *

It is late. The night watch has been on duty for the past three hours. Nonetheless, like any other office building after hours, the NSA office takes on a different personality at night. Perhaps it is the endless screensavers performing their individual twists and turns to an invisible audience in their dimly lit offices that helps create the illusion of timeless motion. The ticking clocks on the walls, like a heartbeat, tap out the building's rhythmic pulse of night-time activities.

For Mitchell, this is nothing new or strange. The NSA listening station where he works in Greenland is used to the rhythm of perpetual dusk for three months of every year. In a sense, working late at night in the metropolis is like daily life north of the Arctic Circle. Even more so tonight, as Mitchell looks out of his office window: it is starting to snow.

"Hey, Mitch!"

Mitchell snaps round at the door and sees Hal Cameron, perhaps the best forensic analyst in the NSA and second only to Sands in solving problems.

"Jesus Christ!" Mitchell barks back.

"Thanks for the promotion, but you can still call me Hal." The trademark Cheshire cat smile erupts across his face. "Great to see you back amongst the warm-blooded again. Obviously, you escaped your igloo and polar bear guards."

Cameron adopts a schoolyard boy impression, wagging his finger at Mitchell with a sway of his hips and a patronising, trill voice.

"Have you been forgiven by the grownups for being a naughty boy now?"

Mitchell stands and quickly moves to the coffee percolator on a corner table of his office.

"What the hell you are doing here this late?"

Mitchell composes himself enough to pour a cup of coffee for Cameron.

Cameron is tending towards the overweight side of the well-built but his five feet eleven inches height mask it well. His reputation for his unique dress sense does not let him down tonight as he wears, with pride, it must be said, a bilious multi-coloured Hawaiian shirt, a worn, brown-coloured corduroy sports jacket and khaki trousers.

"Sands. She called me after you sent down that pencil rubbing from Kensington's desk."

Mitchell hands Cameron his coffee while he moves to take a seat back at his desk.

"Thanks." Cameron takes a sip.

Cameron flops himself down into a soft chair by the door.

"Looks like a suicide note written in Kensington's own handwriting, nothing too dramatic. The calligraphy department report is inconclusive regarding whether he wrote the note freely or if he was made to write it under duress. There is a name in the text that we can't fill in as the combinations are too numerous. We would need to do a full personal trace on him to narrow the possibilities."

"Not his wife or kids' names?" Mitchell had to ask.

"Duh!" Cameron mimicked Homer Simpson. Matt Groening would have been impressed. "Now, why didn't we think of that?"

Despite sarcasm being the lowest form of wit, Mitchell gets the point – he smiles back at Cameron.

"Sorry."

"Here is a facsimile of the note." Cameron hands a piece of paper to Mitchell.

R
Can't tinue. o much pr es knows I need to tal . I
you'll understand.
I'll be ing for you the othersi Be areful e may
after all us John

"This missing word?" Mitchell enquires.

"We're pretty certain it's a name, but there wasn't enough to impression to help us," Cameron explains.

"A name?"

"There's nothing else that would fit easily in the context. It also mentions a 'he' on line three, so it is safe."

"So, we fill in the blank and we'll have our first real lead."

Cameron nods in agreement.

"He was a very depressed individual either way. On a brighter note, I do have something else that might interest you."

"What?" Mitchell's curiosity is piqued further.

"A letter; it arrived for Kensington this morning in Greenbelt."

"A letter?"

"Yeah, a good old boy called Franklin from Greenbelt PD sent it up. Know him?"

"Yeah, Greenbelt PD. I met him."

"Well, he reluctantly sent it up to us via courier today, and guess what? It is post-stamped in Russia – Moscow, in fact. Ooh, spooky, right?"

* * *

Despite the snow on the ground and the slate-coloured sky, it is a beautiful morning, cold and crisp. Mitchell parks his car in the East car park at the metro entrance to the Pentagon. Like many thousands of tourists before him, he pauses momentarily and looks to the Southside section of the Pentagon where, on that fateful day in September 2001, a loaded passenger plane was flown into the building, killing all 189 people on board. Mitchell shakes his head, still in disbelief that his profession had let the nation down on that day.

The security, as he suspected, is vigilant and military in presence. The Pentagon is virtually a city within a city. Approximately 23,000 employees, both military and civilian, work here, and the practised procedures of entering the home of the nation's defence are in evidence as a stream of employees line up to be processed through metal detectors. Mitchell joins a fast-moving queue.

As Mitchell walks through the first detector, it makes a loud and piercing beep, within seconds a pistol is pointing at him. Two serious-looking military policemen walk over to intercept him. Mitchell slowly raises his hands.

"Paul Mitchell, National Security Agency. I do have a weapon."

Although his manner looked calm, the speed at which he utters the words gives away his anxiety. Slowly, Mitchell takes his identification from his jacket and presents it to the closet of the MPs.

"You will have to leave your weapon at reception, sir, and collect it on the way out."

Mitchell lowers his hands and opens his coat to reveal his sidearm, a 9mm colt .45 automatic. The officer takes the weapon and hands it to the desk officer who has now, thankfully, holstered his own pistol.

"I have an appointment to see Dr. Henry Eidelman," Mitchell adds.

"Dr. Eidelman is on the fourth floor, corridor B, room 432. Once you are on the fourth floor, follow the red line marked on the floor to your left. Please use elevator 3 which is located behind you."

The directions are simple and delivered as an order. Mitchell is not about to disobey them.

"Thanks." Mitchell walks to the elevator.

* * *

As Mitchell walks to the elevator, however many times he visits, he cannot help himself but admire the building he is in, wondering how many civilians know the history of such an ostentatious building. Mr. Leslie Groves built it, a name Joe Public, Mitchell surmises, would never have heard. Mitchell continues his daydream thought as he steps inside the elevator, pressing the fourth floor button to take him to Eidelman's office. Leslie Groves, later General Groves of the United States Corps of Engineers, was in fact the mastermind behind the assembly of the world's best atomic scientists for the New Mexico top secret Manhattan Project. The Manhattan Project was where

J. Robert Oppenheimer built and detonated the first atomic bomb. Mitchell concludes, perhaps still not many would have heard about Leslie Groves and his contribution to the United States. Anonymity, in this case, however, is perhaps for the best.

* * *

There are 131 stairways and thirteen elevators in the Pentagon. The building covers twenty-nine acres over five floors requiring 284 restrooms for its 23,000 workforce who park their cars in the sixty-seven acres reserved for employees outside. That was about as far as Mitchell's trivia knowledge went on Washington's behemoth, other than who built it.

Mitchell smiles to himself in a congratulatory way, having still remembered the information. Trivia is something he is good at. A knack he acquired at elementary school in New England. An average student in maths and English, yet in history he was the champ. As he saw it, history was just snippets of trivia to be remembered, so he did that part of his education very well. It was probably this unqualified ability that made him stand out as one of the best NSA investigators in the bureau. Despite his big mouth and poor attitude, he was once considered the best at what he did.

Pondering this particular train of thought takes him exactly the right amount of time to reach the fourth floor and for the doors to open with a ding of satisfaction of a mission accomplished. The red line that he was told about at reception is where it should have been, so he follows it. Room 432 is just a short distance from the elevator. Mitchell notices that the door is slightly ajar. Mitchell knocks and walks in.

The room is a tip, packed full of papers, books, document folders, cups, old lunch boxes and newspaper clippings. On the wall hangs an array of photos of star systems and galaxies, interspersed with the occasional certificate, which all seem to hang askew. A man wearing a light brown cardigan and dark trousers stands with his back to the door. His head is bowed as if in prayer, with his hands hidden in front of his body. Mitchell looks to see if anyone else is in the room before entering further.

Suddenly, the man gently moves to the right and then back to the left.

A rattling sound is heard and then, "Oh, yes!"

"Dr. Eidelman?" Mitchell calls out.

Eidelman turns sharply with a golf putter in his hand and proceeds to knock a pile of papers to the floor.

"Yes! My dear fellow, yes, I'm Eidelman."

A flustered Eidelman extends a hand. Mitchell takes it.

"And you're Martins?"

"Mitchell."

"Of course you are, Michaels. How are you, dear boy? Please come in and make yourself, er, hm."

Eidelman looks around his room as if it were for the first time and is shocked by the mess.

"...Some space."

Mitchell takes another, long look at the man in front of him.

"They don't let me out much, as you probably have guessed, but I do enjoy the game." Eidelman smiles warmly.

"Game?" Mitchell asks with curiosity.

"Golf, Mr. Morton, a game that consists of a lot of walking, broken up by moments of disappointment and bad arithmetic. I simply love it. But to keep ahead of the game, you must practise. Say you understand."

"Of course, and my name is Mitchell. Mitchell."

"I know that."

Eidelman starts to pick up the papers. Mitchell starts to pick up the papers too.

"Let me help you, Doctor."

Mitchell steals an unguarded glance at the doctor. It is uncanny, but Eidelman is a dead ringer for the actor Walter Matthau. It is an incredible likeness.

"Dr. Eidelman?"

"What can I do for you? I'm sure it's not to discuss my handicap. Ms. Sands was a little ambiguous as to your reasons for wanting to see me. I hope it isn't anything too dull. I must admit, her vagueness piqued my curiosity. I'm hoping it will involve some cloak and dagger stuff, you know, James Brooke Bond. Oh, oh, oh dear, I think I got that wrong, didn't I?"

"Nothing too intriguing, I'm afraid. Just a few questions about a colleague of yours."

Eidelman's shoulders visibly sink lower. He sighs.

"Oh, how disappointing. Is that all? Never mind, why don't you take a seat. I was just about to make some coffee; would you like some?"

"Yes, that would be nice, thank you." *At last,* Mitchell thinks, *safe territory.*

Mitchell clears a chair of a pile of papers and takes a seat. The seat is soft, and he sits further and deeper down in the chair than he expected to. He watches as Eidelman moves cautiously through the labyrinth of junk scattered on the floor and precariously balanced on desktops. He heads towards a bookcase that seems to double for a kitchenette.

"I was hoping if you could tell me about Dr. John Kensington." Mitchell speaks loudly; he reasons, irrationally, that Eidelman will be hard of hearing.

"No need to shout, son. Black or white?"

"Sorry, sir. White, one sugar, if you have any."

Mitchell watches Eidelman closely. Eidelman picks up a coffee pot and judges its water content by weight, without looking inside at the level. Eidelman seems satisfied there is enough and unceremoniously drops it on to a nearby hot plate.

"Cups. My life seems to be an endless search for these things!"

Eventually finding two under an old raincoat, Eidelman studies the contents of each carefully, sticking a finger inside one and then, much to Mitchell's ever-increasing doubt of ever accepting the offer of a coffee, sniffs his finger. A shrug of the shoulders indicates it meets his approval.

Eidelman, suddenly realising he is not alone, looks over his shoulder and sees that Mitchell is watching his every move. He smiles disarmingly.

"Do you like those pictures, Mr. Mitchell?"

Mitchell glances across the room at the star field pictures he had seen when he first entered the room. He gets up to look at them closer.

"From the James Webb telescope," Eidelman adds.

Mitchell looks them over. "Very dramatic images."

"No point printing the dull ones, my boy, who'd buy them?"

While Mitchell is looking at the photographs on the wall, Eidelman quickly empties the contents of both mugs over a very ill-looking potted plant propped up in a nearby corner. Taking a quick glance to confirm his guest's preoccupation with the photographs, Eidelman pulls out his shirttail from within his trousers and uses it to wipe out the coffee cups.

"I know John very well."

Mitchell turns.

"I took over from him here, as a matter of fact. I hope he hasn't got himself into any hot water with his CDM radio telescope. You know, eavesdropping on some hush-hush top-secret skullduggery where he shouldn't have?"

"No, nothing like that." Mitchell is warming to Eidelman's eccentric manner.

"I ask as he was known to be a little acrimonious with authority of late. Was never like that when we first met. Became bitter over the years, I think. Should have taken up golf like me. Einstein apparently said, after holing a fifteen-yard putt, 'God does not deduct from our allotted lifespan the time spent playing golf.' And he knew a thing or two about time, that boy."

"Sands didn't tell you then?" Mitchell watches Eidelman's face closely for a reaction to the news he is about to give him. Perhaps it might indicate the state of their relationship.

"Heard what, my boy?" Eidelman prompts.

"I'm afraid Dr. Kensington is dead."

"*No!*" His reaction is immediate and natural.

Mitchell continues, "Two days ago. We believe he committed suicide."

"Good Lord, do you know why?"

The hot water for the coffee begins to boil over, breaking the stillness of the moment as the water spits and hisses. Eidelman turns and removes it from the heat.

"I was hoping you could help us with that." Mitchell watches closely as Eidelman absorbs the information as he adds, "The only indication of his mental state is from his resignation letter. He seemed disillusioned, even confused, especially with his work at the institute and project CDM, which he headed before coming here."

Eidelman looks at him. "His resignation wasn't totally unexpected, so they tell me. We were all disillusioned towards the end of that year," Eidelman adds as an afterthought.

"All?" Mitchell is surprised to hear this.

"Yes, all the science community I'm talking about. The vagaries of politicians looking for the popular vote have always been and shall always be the bane of the scientific community. The swings and balances of the latest administration saw the end of John's project over at Goddard and numerous others nationwide. Nothing new there; the Manhattan Project, the Apollo Space Programme and the Strategic Defence Initiative were all casualties of the same cut-and-run policy in the past, you see. Now the new money is in climate prediction, global dimming, AI research, the greenhouse effect. It's on the world agenda and about time too, don't get me wrong! We have been yelling at the top of our voices for decades that the world was on the edge of a climatic precipice. A natural cycle or manmade or both, the argument was too broad to be taken seriously, until, that is, people started dying. Look at poor New Orleans in 2005. They knew it would happen.

"Hurricanes are inevitable, with greater ferocity. Floods in one part of the world, fires and droughts in another. Heatwaves and cold snaps are making the front pages worldwide. Only when famine and crop failure in the West is mooted did the politicians sit up and take notice. Too late, of course, but they now fear losing their precious votes. Pop goes the funding for the less popular sciences to placate the masses. And what do we do about it? Zip, nada is what! Science has always been a complicated business."

Eidelman turns and puts two spoonfuls of instant coffee into each mug. Mitchell's first impression of Eidelman as a bumbling academic is now quickly changing. His assessment of the plight of his fellow professional scientists is acute. He has his finger on the pulse of his community and knows how it works, the symbiotic relationship between politicians and voters far outweighing the pure scientist on the treadmill of discovery.

Turning back to face Mitchell, Eidelman continues, "You see, Mr. Mitchell, we scientists are not the most virtuous of people. We tend to align ourselves with any current thinking, if the funding is adequate to quell any moral misgivings we might have. When the appropriations started to run out for the Apollo programme, we simply began to look elsewhere for our next meal ticket. The Space Shuttle came along. Okay, the shuttle was a compromise. It was not what the great Maxime Faget conceived or designed as our next manned space flight system."

"Faget?"

"Yes, Max Faget, the father of manned space flight. He passed away a disappointed soul in 2004." Eidelman sighs. "Anyway, while the Cold War lasted, we were in the groove, so my younger research colleagues tell me is the correct lingo."

Eidelman finally offers Mitchell a cup of coffee.

"Thanks." Mitchell takes the cup and sips the coffee carefully from a clean part of the cup rim, of which there aren't many.

"However, John was never as licentious as the rest of us." Eidelman sits down in an old, cracked leather chair, sips his coffee and recoils at the taste. Looking at the cup, he wipes a smudge of grime from the rim. "Of course, we all realised that the Strategic Defence Initiative was a hopeless dream and never had the chance of becoming a working reality. It was simply a dealmaker used by Reagan in Reykjavik. Its premise was a military answer to a political problem, and how many times have you known that to work?"

"Not wanting to stray too far from the point here," Mitchell had a republican head, but a democratic heart, "but it did work, Doctor. Reagan convinced the Soviets into thinking that their nuclear missiles would become obsolete when SDI came into operation. They couldn't afford to develop their own system. It would have broken their economy, so they came to the negotiating table. It won the Cold War."

Giving up on foul-tasting coffee, Eidelman pours the contents of his cup into the nearby, over-abused flowerpot containing the sickly plant he watered earlier.

"But what surprised us," Eidelman continues, "was that the Soviets fell for it, hook, line, and sinker. They knew that we could never track all the warheads coming into US airspace, let alone be able to destroy them before they reached their targets. Not only that, but they could also under fly the whole system with ground-skimming tactical nuclear weapons, like our own Tomahawk cruise missiles. The Soviets must have known all this. Maybe they were just looking for an excuse to cut their military's power. Who knows?"

"As background, this is very useful, of course, but could we —"

"John!" Eidelman cuts Mitchell short. "Of course, poor John. Sorry about all that."

"Do you know of any personal problems he may have had?" Mitchell moves the conversation quickly on.

"We never talked much about his personal life. It was common knowledge that he and his wife were having difficulties, but when he moved to Goddard to head up CDM, it all seemed to get a lot better."

"Because?" Mitchell looked for clarification.

"The gossip stopped." Eidelman smiles. "I'm not one for gossip, can't seem to remember the juicy bits. Our conversations were mainly about work."

"Dedicated?" Mitchell added.

"You have to be," Eidelman retorted.

Eidelman was right, of course. The competition for the limited funds available in non-commercial science means that you needed to stay on top of your game twenty-four-seven. Mitchell shared empathy of sorts with Eidelman. When he joined the NSA, he was the brightest star in the agency; now college kids are swamping the agency with their double doctorates and high IQs. To be a player today, you need to be dedicated.

"Did he ever mention a person called Karl?"

Eidelman reaches into his cardigan pocket and pulls out a pipe.

"There was a scientist, Karl Hunter I think that was his name, who worked on CDM with John. John spoke highly of him. Might be your man."

Mitchell makes a note on a pad he pulls from the inside of his jacket pocket.

"Where would I find this Karl Hunter now?" As Mitchell looks back to Eidelman, he can see him attempting to fill his pipe from a tartan tobacco pouch.

"Don't mind, do you?" Eidelman asks, not really caring what the answer would be.

"No, please do," Mitchell replies.

Eidelman lights the pipe with a Zippo lighter. Big clouds of smoke billow about his head.

"Clan Pipe Tobacco," Eidelman adds, "loved the smell as a child. My father used to smoke it."

Mitchell soon smells the sweet, distinctive aroma of the tobacco.

"No idea, sorry." Eidelman pulls the pipe from his mouth to speak and waves his other hand to clear some of the smoke.

A loud beeping sound comes from Mitchell's jacket pocket. Pulling his mobile, Mitchell scans the LED display.

"Excuse me, Doctor, I need to take a call. This is Mitchell." There's a pause while Mitchell listens. "I'll be there immediately." He hangs up. "I'm sorry, Dr. Eidelman, I must go. Thanks for the coffee and here's my contact details. If you think of anything that might help, anything at all, please call me on this number."

Eidelman stands and offers Mitchell his hand.

Chapter Four

Hal Cameron stubs out a cigarette in an already overflowing ashtray that sits on his desk. Cameron had been smoking since he was an adolescent. He was putting on weight in high school and everyone knew back then that fat kids rarely got girls. He needed as much help as he could muster on that front. Smoking, he once read in a magazine, helps to sate the appetite, so he took up smoking to lose weight. Now in his mid-forties and a chain-smoking blubber magnet, he could honestly say what a cartload of horse manure that article really was. He'll give up smoking and go on a diet… next year.

The office door opens.

"Mitch? That you?" Cameron's voice is raspy at best tonight: too many cigarettes, even by his standard.

"Hal, why the hell don't you ever open a window or turn on a fan?" Mitchell frantically waves his hand in front of his face.

"It must be twenty below out there!" Cameron wheezes. "Didn't you hear the weather report on the news this morning? It's going to be a whiteout of a Christmas." Cameron starts to sing the first few lines of 'White Christmas'.

Mitchell dumps his coat and briefcase on a side table and

takes a seat at his desk. Cameron's smoker's cough soon draws to a close his unique rendition of the Christmas favourite.

"You hear about the suicide bombings in London?" Cameron splutters.

"Yeah, on the way in. Looks worse than 07/07/05." Mitchell shakes his head. "The world is going to hell in a hand cart!"

"Scotland Yard is saying radical clerics are openly encouraging it." Cameron coughs hard once again. Mitchell looks painfully across at his friend struggling to catch his breath.

"Why not make an early New Year's resolution, Hal? Give up smoking: it would be healthier for all of us."

Cameron sighs and stubs out another cigarette. "Thanks."

Mitchell turns on a desk fan and a cloud of smoke heads for the open door.

"Your call made it sound pretty urgent, what have you found?"

Cameron picks up a white sheet of paper that is beside him.

"That letter from Russia made for some interesting reading. I probably lost some of the flavour in the translation, but basically it strikes me as a letter written by a very distressed individual to an old friend."

Cameron hands Mitchell the translation.

"Was it signed?" Mitchell asks before looking at the transcript.

"Yes, it was, by Anton Medvedenko. Heard of him?"

"No, should I have?"

"Not really. He's a Russian national who worked as part of a small international scientific project. Some of the work was based here in the States. We're still checking. I've asked records for a reference search, correlating his name with that of John Kensington."

"Eidelman suggested we check out Karl Hunter. Add that to the list too."

"He thinks it might be Karl in the note?" Cameron speculates.

"It's a possibility; they worked together, as you know, six years ago, on the CDM project," Mitchell clarifies the link for Cameron.

Cameron lights another cigarette.

"All in all, Kensington seems to have been a perfect candidate for recruitment by a foreign agency." Mitchell rotates the desk fan towards Cameron. "A loner with high ideals and a chip on his shoulder."

"Maybe we should have hired him ourselves." Cameron inhales deeply, making the end of his cigarette glow fiercely in the added downdraft from the fan.

"Maybe. It's probably going to take records a while to recover those files, so how about a bite to eat? I have skipped several sit-down meals these past few days."

"Not for me, Mitch, I'm trying to lose weight." Cameron places the lighted cigarette into his mouth with one hand and taps his pot belly with the other hand, adding, "New Year's resolutions coming up."

"Getting a head start, huh?" Mitchell laughs. "You have to look after yourself, you know."

Mitchell looks incredulously at Cameron as he stands, grabs his coat and leaves.

* * *

The Moscow district of Frunzenskaya sits on an embankment, just across the Moskva River from Gorky Park in what is now a Putin-era, post-Glasnost, middle-class suburb. Streetlamps cast a grey hue over a few parked cars outside closed shops. Red graffiti paint drips over the metal shutters, shouting: *STOP THE WAR IN UKRAINE*. The only touch of colour in an otherwise dank, empty road. Hard-packed, dirty snow covers the street as the night-time temperature pauses temporarily at -8°C.

Four state militia police cars pull up silently and stop outside a typical Stalin-era house. With little urgency, the occupants – six policemen in dress uniform and a civilian – get out of their cars. They stand on the pavement, looking up at the house. Their breath, frozen as soon as it leaves their mouths, hangs in the air like vapours from plastic cigarettes.

The tallest of the policemen, a broad, burly Muscovite with a cluster of gold oak leaves on his shoulders, climbs the six steps to the front door of a nearby house, while his colleagues wait on the pavement below.

He bangs loudly on the door with a clenched fist and shouts, "*Откройтесь. Это – полиция!*"

To a generation of Russian citizens born during Stalin's reign of terror, those simple words shouted in the middle of the night conjure up a nightmare. 'Open up, it's the police' could mean it was your family about to be exiled to Siberia by morning, stripped of possessions, clothes, shoes, money, even food, and bundled into a van to be taken to a railway station for immediate deportation to oblivion. Reasons unknown.

For those born later, nothing much has changed. Those memories only serve as a way of educating the Russian populace of the facts of life.

"*Откройтесь. Это – полиция!*"

Curtains twitch as neighbours cautiously observe the drama being played outside their homes. No reply. The officer signals his colleagues to join him. With little discussion, the door is kicked open and three militia police officers storm in, all with weapons drawn.

The tall officer tries switching on the lights, but there is no power. Flashlights are soon produced, their light piercing the darkness as the officers begin to search the downstairs area of the house.

There is a smell, bittersweet in nature, but the cold air is making it hard to distinguish. One of the flashlights catches a glimpse of something on a wall, a little way inside the hall, which needs a closer look. A junior ranking office is signalled forward to investigate.

"*Это – кровь, Командующий.*"

"What did he say?" The civilian speaks in an American voice! He looks to the commander for a translation.

The commander is surprised by what his junior officer has told him. In a heavy Russian accent, he translates for his American colleague.

"He says there is blood."

The commander looks for himself.

In fact, the wall is splattered with blood.

"*Здесь, Командующий,*" another militia officer calls the attention of his commander to a room off the main entrance way.

"*Здесь, Командующий.*"

The commander walks to where his officer is standing, the American following closely behind. The commander walks to the room, his flashlight marking the way forward.

"I think it's the kitchen," the commander relays to the American. A large pool of congealed blood covers the black-and-white checkered flooring. A trail of blood leads out of the kitchen and back into the entrance hall. Flashlights follow the trail that ends at the foot of the stairs.

The commander leads his men to the foot of the stairs and, with the flashlight in one hand and a Browning .9mm semi-automatic pistol in the other, he looks up the stairs to a dark top landing.

There is more blood on the top stairs and walls.

"Careful, men," the commander warns his men in English as he leads the way up the stairs. His fellow officers take offensive covering positions just behind him.

At the top of the stairs, the commander quickly scans the area with his flashlight. Two doors can clearly be seen, the closest door is partially open and the second is closed. The commander signals his men to move in and take positions at the doors. Taking the closest door first, the commander, followed by the American observer, moves into position.

The bittersweet odour becomes potent again as they pass nearby the closest door. Pausing only to check that his men are all armed and ready, the commander slowly opens the door to the room, his pistol ready.

It is a child's room. Toys are scattered around the floor, covered in blood splats. The bed is neatly made; children's drawings of planets and moons hang on the wall. Otherwise, the room is empty. No cupboards.

"What in Christ's name happened here?" The American coughs and slaps his hand over his nose and mouth, trying in vain to stop the stench of blood reaching his senses.

Turning, the commander signals his men to move on to the next room.

In the corridor, the commander signals one of his officers to open the next door. It is locked. Taking one step back, he gains momentum and kicks the door open with his heavy boot. The door bursts open and he quickly moves to one side, allowing another officer room to fire if attacked. Silence greets them. The commander arrives quickly and shines his flashlight into the room.

The flashlights of the officers reflect light back into their faces and there, on each face, an expression of revulsion and bloody horror is illuminated.

* * *

Mitchell clears the condensation from the window, using the paper napkin given to him with his order of Grande cappuccino and toasted Swiss cheese on rye. The view from this little coffee house, on the corner of Constitution Avenue and 15th Street, is the best in the Capitol, overlooking the park and the Washington Monument. Rising 555 feet into the air, as a tribute to the first president, it still demands Mitchell's attention, even though he had visited the Capitol, on and off, all his working life.

Taking a large bite out of his sandwich, Mitchell looks back out at the vista in front of him to see the comical sight of Hal Cameron negotiating his body between a parked postal office truck and a police car. The gap is too small. One or other of them is going to have to give way as Cameron squeezes and wriggles his body between the temporary blockades.

Thankfully for Mitchell's digestion, the postal truck moves off down 15th Street, allowing Cameron a fleeting triumph of man over machine. Mitchell catches the attention of a waitress.

"Miss, could I have another cappuccino, please? No smoking here, right?"

"That's right, sir. No smoking on the premises," the waitress says with a smile as she walks away to fetch the coffee order.

Mitchell watches Cameron bustle in from outside. Cameron searches for Mitchell, soon spots him, and makes his way to where he is sitting. Cameron flops down on a seat opposite Mitchell. Cameron is puffing and wheezing. He looks up at Mitchell who is smiling broadly back at him.

"Wait just one God damn minute," Cameron croaks, taking a packet of Camel brand cigarettes from his shirt pocket. Mitchell grabs his hand. He points to a large sign with his other hand that reads: NO SMOKING.

"Ah shit. What about my rights? This is a *woke* world we live in, for sure. D.C. is a smoke-free zone these days." Cameron is furious. "Obviously, except my office!"

Mitchell smiles broadly.

"Here you go, sir." The waitress delivers the coffee.

"Thank you," both say in chorus.

"What brings you out into the fresh air?" Mitchell enquires earnestly.

"I've got some information regarding Medvedenko that I thought you might like to see."

"And you came all this way; I'm touched."

"You will be. I decided to take you up on your offer of lunch – you're paying, of course."

"Diet lasted about thirty minutes; same as the last diet you were on then?" Mitchell quips back.

"Medvedenko is indeed back living in Moscow." Cameron takes a file from a folder he had placed on the table and reads from the paper he extracted, "With his family in a suburb called Frunzenskaya."

"Near Gorky Park, I know of it," Mitchell adds casually. Cameron is most impressed at this but hides it from him.

"Yeah, near Gorky Park. Well, he and his family have been there since CDM folded. This is a CIA briefing file so it's fairly sketchy. Anyway, we still don't know if or when he worked with Kensington. The last project Medvedenko worked on was – are you ready for this? – CDM. When the funding ran out, he went back to Russia."

Mitchell is beginning to see a picture; he just needs to find all the bits of the puzzle.

"What did Medvedenko specialise in?"

"Cosmology and physics; apparently he is well known in those fields."

"Do we know where he is working now?"

"No, but he was attached to the Academy of Russian Sciences. They've even got a PR office now, so we could give them a call and ask."

"It's not as much fun as it used to be, is it? I mean, we call them up and ask now instead of—"

"Cloak and dagger stuff?" Cameron interjects.

"Investigative analysis is what I was going to say."

"They could still lie to us," Cameron adds, smiling.

Mitchell laughs as he looks at his watch. "There's no chance of them lying to us at the moment; eight hours ahead, vodka and borsch time in Moscow right now. We'll give them a call first thing in the morning – they can lie to us then."

Mitchell stands and collects his coat from the vacant seat next to him.

"This CDM project must have been funded with US dollars, so I'll pay a visit to the people at the Bureau of Scientific Records, see if they've got anything on Medvedenko and CDM. You go back to the office after lunch and start digging around. I want all the information you can find on Kensington's past work. There must be a link here somewhere between Kensington, Medvedenko, and this Karl person. And I think our answer lies with whoever this 'blank' person is in the suicide note."

Mitchell pulls the collar up on his coat in preparation for the cold blast you get when leaving an air-conditioned building in midwinter.

"If I find anything, I'll call you."

The waitress comes back to the table and stands ready to take Cameron's food order.

"Chicken fried steak, eggs over easy, crispy bacon and a stack of your best pancakes, smothered in Canadian maple syrup, please."

"Thank you." The waitress takes the menu from Cameron and leaves.

Mitchell smiles and shakes his head. "*Bon appetite*, my friend."

* * *

The offices of the Bureau of Scientific Records are housed in an imposing stone-clad building on Connecticut Avenue, near Fort Reno Park, Washington, D.C. The building, when in its prime, was the grandiose headquarters of the scientific elite of America and this was reflected in its architecture.

For Mitchell, the building reminds him of the great south front of his favourite museum, the British Museum in London. Greek Revival in style, with majestic columns, similar in design to Sir Robert Smirke's façade on Great Russell Street. However, unlike its London counterpart, the Bureau sticks out like a sore thumb in the clatter of modern edifices that encompass it today.

Tarnished by pollution and prematurely aged by neglect, Mitchell still feels he is entering a building that houses great knowledge and wisdom, something Mitchell never felt when visiting the Smithsonian at 600 Maryland Avenue, D.C. – same city, different vibes, for Mitchell anyway.

The interior of the building is no less imposing. *Cavernous*, is how Mitchell silently observes the splendid open space of the main entrance lobby. A grand stone staircase leads visitors to the first floor where Mitchell sees, for the first time, people milling about. The building's interior is cold, unheated, and Mitchell can still see his breath, although he is a good twenty metres inside the lobby. At the foot of the grand staircase, there is a building occupancy guide. Scanning the plastic clip-on letters, he quickly finds the office he needs – first floor west, the Benjamin Franklin Room.

Directions on the first floor are surprisingly easy to follow and Mitchell soon finds the Franklin room. Knocking on the ornate, panelled wooden door, he waits for a reply. Nothing. Regardless, he enters. Mitchell is surprised by the size and grandeur of the room concealed by the wooden door he has just opened. The room is huge, divided into long corridors of impressively stocked bookcases. Shafts of light illuminate the room from tall stained glass windows, high up in the walls. The elaborate detailing of the master glaziers illustrates significant events in scientific American history, including, Mitchell notes, Benjamin Franklin's kite flying.

Below Franklin's window is the reception desk where a studious-looking man in his late forties is preoccupied with a manuscript in front of him. Mitchell stands unnoticed in front of him for several moments.

Glancing at the manuscript, Mitchell can see that it is in fact an ancient ledger. The ledger is entitled 'Liber B'.

"'Liber B'?" Although Mitchell speaks quietly, as if in a library, the man reading the ledger is startled and jumps.

"Sorry if I startled you," Mitchell adds quickly.

"Oh, that's alright. Didn't think the old ticker could beat any faster. You proved me wrong. Got lost in my hobby again, old habit, wife hates it." The man closes the book.

"Paul Mitchell, NSA." Mitchell produces his ID. "I was just curious as to the manuscript you are reading?"

"Professor Peter Jones, nice to meet you. Ah, the ledger! Well, what a story there, Mr. Mitchell. I love all things mysterious, don't you?"

Before Mitchell could reply, Jones interjects, "Of course you do, you're NSA, silly question. I have a fondness for silly questions, Mr. Mitchell, as the answers are usually the truth. Complicated questions require complicated replies, and I can't be bothered with those."

Mitchell detects an English accent, undoubtedly blunted by years of indoctrination by the American 'bastardised' version. Like the last redcoat at the Battle of Yorktown, his accent is fighting a futile engagement; the inevitable surrender to General George Washington's overwhelming army will soon wash away all trace of his native tongue from his lips.

"'Liber B' is a Masonic manuscript. The oldest Masonic artifact in the United States, I believe. A ledger of members and payments to the Masonic Grand Lodge of Pennsylvania, and it's over 270 years old. Do you have time to hear about my little hobby, Mr. Mitchell? No one really comes here anymore, so if I rabbit on a bit… do you understand?"

"Please, go on." *Why not?* Mitchell thinks. A distraction might help clear his mind. After all, his body clock is still back in Greenland, and this might give it a chance to catch up a bit.

"Oh goodie!" Jones turns a page of the manuscript and Mitchell takes a seat in front of his desk. "The origins of this ledger date back to 1730; the significance is obvious."

It is? Mitchell asks himself silently.

"Because one hundred years after this was written, around 1830, a man named William Morgan published an exposé of Masonic rituals. I have a copy at home; fascinating stuff. Anyway, soon after its publication, he vanished."

"Vanished?" Mitchell reiterates.

"Yes, completely. Neither family nor friends ever hear from him again," Jones continues. "It was widely believed at the time that he was murdered by the Masons for revealing their secrets. Can you imagine it? A secret society with rituals, capable of kidnappings, perhaps even murder, to keep their secrets safe! Well, you can imagine the public outcry. Overwhelming. In fact, so much so, a third political party was formed, in addition to the standard Republican and Democratic fare we have today: the Anti-Masonic Party."

"Really? I never knew that." Mitchell is learning something new.

"Indeed. Masonic members were blacklisted, like the communists of the McCarthy era. They were hunted down and put on public trial. Friends informed on friends, family members on family members. Like a Salem witch hunt really, and that's why the Masonic movement in America went underground, so to speak. No one was to utter another word for decades about their secret society for fear of retribution. Even to this day, certain rituals are considered taboo for public digest."

"Fascinating." Mitchell is pleasantly surprised to learn of this hidden history.

"Oh, popular conspiracy fodder, I grant you, but these tantalising snippets of actual evidence, still stoke the fires of one's imagination."

Jones taps the pages of the ledger.

"It makes for a great investigative hobby – the study of secret societies." Jones smiles broadly.

"And why is the book here and not in the National Archive?"

"A good question, Mr. Mitchell." Jones lowers his voice as if he was about to utter a top-secret code of supreme national importance, but his own enthusiasm for his hobby cannot contain his excitement.

"The room you are now standing in is the Benjamin Franklin room, named in honour of the great American scientist and diplomat. In this ledger is an entry detailing his membership and contribution details to the Grand Lodge of Pennsylvania. The name Benjamin Franklin is right here, look."

Jones points to an entry. Mitchell looks at the point indicated.

"Benjamin Franklin was one of the first Freemasons in America and would have been a marked man if he had been born just one hundred years later. Like a McCarthy communist, he would have been blacklisted from public life, perhaps never fulfilling his providence, never becoming an ambassador to the Court of St. James in England."

"Or have a room in the Bureau of Scientific Records named after him," Mitchell adds.

"Precisely. Ha! History plays some funny games, don't you think, Mr. Mitchell? Now, what can I do for you?"

"I need information on a scientific project which finished six years ago. It was based in Greenbelt, Maryland." Mitchell glances at the rows upon rows of documents and books about them. "Can you help?"

"Six years ago, you say. Those files will still be on paper record. I must put all this on computer files. Books are old hat, it seems, but not a very quick process, as you can imagine. Hence my little hobby breaks; stems the tide of boredom. Job for life, they told me when I took the post. What a life!"

Jones rises from behind his desk and heads towards a row of shelves. Together they walk down one of the long isles of bookcases.

"The six-year-old records are kept down here."

Jones studies the catalogue labels on the shelves as they pass by. Mitchell keeps pace behind him, as Jones looks from one shelf to another.

"The project was called CDM," Mitchell offers in a hope it will help and speed things up a bit.

"Do you know what the acronym stands for?" Jones asks.

"Sorry, no." Mitchell feels useless.

"Never mind, I should still be able to track it down for you."

Jones stops abruptly in front of a large bookcase; Mitchell almost collides with him but manages to pull short. The bookcase is full of files of various sizes and colours.

"Hmm." Jones traces his fingers over their spines, before stopping at a large orange file, which he retrieves from the shelf.

The file is very tattered in appearance. Pulling it from the shelf causes the rest of the files to fall like dominoes, leaving them resting untidily on each other.

"Here we are, Project CDM." Jones places the file on a nearby empty desk and opens it. "It looks like we have just the published material here."

Jones turns the pages looking for more immediate information. Mitchell looks at Jones, who is bent over the table scrupulously studying the manuscripts, mumbling to himself as he turns the pages back and forth. Mitchell looks on a little impatiently, eager to look at the documents himself.

"Ah, here we are. CDM is the acronym for Cold Dark Matter."

"Cold what?" Mitchell is caught unawares by the sudden rush of information. Jones hands Mitchell a section from the file.

"Dark Matter. Is that any help?"

Mitchell looks down the file's index.

"Do you have any idea what that means or what type of research?"

"It should say in these publications, otherwise the Science Grant Allocations Unit should be able to tell you more. They must have supplied the initial funding for the project."

"Is there a list of the scientists involved in this file?"

"Let me see." Jones begins to rummage around in the index of the file. "Ah, here we are." He hands Mitchell a piece of paper.

"What about photographs?" Mitchell studies the list.

"Well, there usually is." Jones looks through the file quickly.

"Hmm. There seems to be a lot of the usual information missing from here. How odd. Seems to be made up of mostly mundane technical material."

Mitchell reads down the list further.

=DR. JOHN KENSINGTON, PROF. ANTON MEDVEDENKO, DR. KARL HUNTER,

RACHEL SIMMONS (Miss)=

His eyes focus on the name of Rachel Simmons.

"Thank you, Professor Jones. This is most helpful."

"Pleased I could be of service."

The two men head back to the reception area where they first met.

"If the records bureau can be of any further help, then please don't hesitate to call."

Jones smiles and waves a farewell to Mitchell.

"Thank you, I will."

Mitchell turns and heads for the door.

* * *

Striding purposefully down the last few stone steps outside the Bureau of Scientific Records, Mitchell scans the road for a taxi. Within moments, a taxi zooms into view and a sharp whistle stops it by the curb.

"Where to?" the taxi driver automatically calls out.

"Treasury building." Mitchell slams the door shut just in time as the taxi pulls away into traffic.

The radio is on: "*This is WBAL 1090 News & Talk Radio – This is Jules Vernon. The situation in Iran with its nuclear enrichment programme has now moved to the United Nations Security Council, in New York, for resolution. Russia and China are the only two permanent members refusing to take part in the negotiations.*"

"Hey, could you turn that down, buddy?"

The driver turns the radio down.

Mitchell reaches inside his coat pocket and retrieves his mobile phone. Flipping open the cover, he presses a quick-dial number and waits for the connection.

The phone on Hal Cameron's desk rings loudly to no avail as the office is empty. Defiantly, the phone continues to ring until it can no longer be ignored. Hal Cameron aimlessly walks in and answers the ringing phone. The taxi suddenly breaks sharply, and Mitchell slides forward on his seat. The driver shouts expletives, in a language Mitchell recognises as Turkish, at a pedestrian who obviously has just had a near call.

"Sorry, mister. You would think a bright yellow cab would be easy to see, huh?"

Mitchell ignores the driver as he sits back in his seat and braces himself with one foot against the dividing partition.

"Hal, it's me. Listen, I have another name for you, get this down: Rachel Simmons. Yes, a woman. She was a team leader along with Kensington, Medvedenko and Hunter on a project called CDM, that is the acronym for…" Mitchell falls briefly silent.

"That's right, Cold Dark Matter, I'm impressed. Listen, drop what you're doing and find her. I'm certain she'd know who or what 'blank' is. And, Hal, find out what you can do about the Science Grant Allocations Unit, then get me an appointment with the head of the unit. Say 'NSA business', that will get you past the receptionist. These people should have some more information about CDM."

Hal Cameron's shorthand was never his forte and his notes look like a drunken pigeon had stumbled into an inkwell and gone for a stroll across his desk.

"Yes, sir, and do I get a pay raise for becoming your secretary? Yeah right. The Science Allocations Unit, got it. Listen, Mitch…" Cameron picks up a piece of telex paper from his desk and reads from it. "We got a wire from our Moscow bureau about ten minutes ago. Anton Medvedenko is dead. The Moscow Militia aren't saying much but the local news agency is calling the scene a massacre. Looks like he killed his entire family, kids as well, before topping himself." Cameron listens for a response. "Mitch, you there?"

The taxi has stopped at a red traffic signal and, as he absorbs the news of the Medvedenko massacre of a young family, parents with two children wait patiently to cross the road. Mitchell can't help but note how happy they seem, in their own little world, oblivious to what Mitchell has just been told.

"When?" Mitchell asks.

Cameron looks at the telex again in his hand. "Within the last few hours."

Mitchell switches off his mobile phone and looks out of the car taxi window, puzzled and a little shaken. It begins to snow again.

* * *

Unlike the Bureau of Scientific Records, the Treasury Offices that host the Science Grant Allocation Unit are in a modern soulless glass block, uninspiring but functional. The taxi pulls up directly outside and, like most government buildings in Washington post-9/11, a policeman approaches to wave the taxi immediately on after dropping off their passengers.

The Science Grant Allocations Unit is located on the seventh floor and, in comparison to the Benjamin Franklin room, these offices are tiny. Although small, Mitchell is impressed with the décor. Large prints of various scientific images hang on the wall, including a research ship at sea, a shuttle launch, the Earth and the Moon as viewed from space, and several Hubble and James Webb telescope images. A leather sofa and coffee table occupy one half of the office, while a career secretary holds court directly opposite.

"Paul Mitchell, NSA." Mitchell reflects that this introduction usually gets him to the front of the queue.

"Yes, I know. I had a call about you. Take a seat and I'll see what I can do for you. But you should really make an appointment at least twenty-four hours in advance."

The tone of her voice is not threatening or discourteous; nonetheless, Mitchell feels scolded. He stands his ground.

"Miss, this is NSA business; I don't require an appointment," he says firmly and, he thinks, with charm.

"Hmm. Well, like I said, take a seat, Mr. Mitchell, and I'll see what I can do for you."

Now Mitchell knows he is dismissed. This is one battle Mitchell could win if he really wanted to. He chooses not to this time and sits down on the sofa in reception.

The magazines on the coffee table are what you would expect in an office for a science unit: *Astronomy*, *National Geographic*, *Scientific American*, and *Nature*, but unlike your average dentist or doctor's waiting room, they are all recent issues. Picking up the *National Geographic*, he glances up at the secretary and smiles. Nothing, no reaction.

"Oh well." Mitchell sighs. *No need to amend my Christmas card list for next year then*, he thinks.

The intercom on the secretary's desk buzzes. Pressing the flashing button, she speaks.

"Yes, Professor?"

"I'll see him now, Miss Bunker."

Mitchell can't help but overhear and, somehow, that name just seems to fit her like a glove.

"I'll send him in right away," she adds.

Turning the intercom back to standby, Miss Bunker looks over and smiles coldly at Mitchell.

"Professor Lawrence will see you now."

For one fleeting moment, Mitchell thinks to say, "Let me just finish this article first, be with you in a minute," but he doesn't.

Mitchell stands and walks towards a door marked 'PRIVATE' directly behind her desk. Knocking once, and not waiting for a reply, he walks in.

* * *

Professor Simon Lawrence rises from behind his desk to greet Mitchell, his hand extended, with a warm smile. The welcome is genuine. Lawrence is tall, complementing his trim physique. Dressed in a smart Herringbone tweed three-piece suit with grey hair and moustache marks him out as a very distinguished figure. Mitchell shakes his hand in greeting.

"Pleased to meet you, Mr. Mitchell. Please take a seat."

Lawrence motions to a seat directly in front of his desk.

"I'm Simon Lawrence, Director of the SGAU. I have to say, it's very unusual for us to get a visitor from your side of the street."

"Which side is that, Professor?" Mitchell asks.

"Homeland Security, isn't it?"

"NSA," Mitchell corrects.

"Oh, I think you're the first agent I've ever met. I must admit, I'm a bit apprehensive."

Although he says he is, Mitchell suspects that Lawrence is acting.

"No need to be, honestly." Mitchell smiles reassuringly. "We just need some information; your unit might be able to help, that's all." Mitchell adds, "We're interested in some background information concerning a project called CDM that closed down about six years ago."

"Yes, a Mr. Cameron called and said that is what you were looking for." Lawrence refers to a notebook on his desk.

"So, Miss Bunker out there was wrong: I do have an appointment."

Lawrence has no comment and shows no expression on his face at Mitchell's knocking of his secretary.

Mitchell continues, "It's the personnel who worked on it rather than the project itself that particularly interests us."

"Oh really, anyone specific?"

It isn't so much his reply but his manner that alerts Mitchell to treat Lawrence with caution. He may not be all he claims to be. Mitchell enters the game Lawrence has just fired the starting pistol on.

"The team leaders mainly. We have accounted for most of the technicians who worked on the project. However, any information you may have on John Kensington, Anton Medvedenko, Karl Hunter, and Rachel Simmons would speed our inquiries."

"I can tell you now that our records will only show the people who worked on the CDM project, and you seem to know most of that already. The remaining staff, I believe, were all made up of research students."

"What about histories, relationships?" Mitchell is disappointed with Lawrence's reply. What is Lawrence hiding? "Professor Jones at Records seemed certain I would find what I was looking for here."

"Really? That surprises me. No, as far as any relationships go, other than professional, our files would be of little help. We deal with professional credentials and only then in terms of funding. A glorified bank loan is what we offer, credentials being the surety."

"I would appreciate any information you have."

"Of course, but I wouldn't expect too much from the files we have here, Mr. Mitchell. You must remember that when this Unit funds a project, it is only really interested in results, however they are obtained. We leave the ethics of science to the National Academy of Sciences. We've found the best way of achieving goals is to leave the scientists to their own devices, any interference by us seems only to lead to resentment."

"Funding with no strings attached, sounds too good to be true," Mitchell observes. "Where's the payback for you?"

"It doesn't work exactly like that, Mr. Mitchell. Perhaps if I could explain better. Approximately forty per cent of the scientific work undertaken in the world today is for a reason, a search for an answer to a specific problem – health, civil engineering, that kind of thing. Payback, as you call it, comes in the form of treatments or cures over which the government would hold licenses."

"I see, and the other sixty per cent?"

"Well, fifty-five per cent or so is military research, weapons manufacture, defence, communications technology, you know, for use on the battlefield, rocket propulsion systems and so on. Less than five per cent is pure investigative work. Science undertaken not knowing what the outcome will be – like CDM, for example."

"Really?"

"Yes, and it is a competitive market. Scientists are not overall a bunch of nutty professors, cooking up magical compounds to make cars fly or the high school basketball team invincible. They are working to deadlines and need results to fund the next phase of their work."

"And you judge each application on percentages?" Mitchell concludes.

"Not entirely. We take the view that a well-funded astronomy project has as much chance of developing techniques or equipment that would justify the taxpayer's trust in our decision to fund the project or projects."

"What about CDM?" Mitchell is curious.

"Of course, if you need to know how much funding the CDM programme used in its operational stage, that would be in the files. But anything concerning the internal workings of the project is beyond this department's knowledge or remit."

"Well, I'm sure what you do have will be of some help to us. I would like to take a copy of the CDM project file with me. Would that be a problem, Professor?"

Mitchell watches carefully for Lawrence's reaction.

"I was only told you would like to see the file. However, I'm sure we can rustle you up a copy, Agent Mitchell."

There is something Mitchell can't quite put a finger on, but Lawrence is hiding something more than just a file.

"I'll get my secretary to prepare the file for you immediately." Lawrence smiles.

"Thank you." Mitchell gathers his coat while Lawrence speaks into the intercom.

"Miss Bunker, could you prepare a complete dossier on Project CDM and have it ready for Agent Mitchell to take away with him?"

Miss Bunker's voice is somehow even more caustic over the airwaves.

"Certainly, Professor."

Lawrence surreptitiously studies Mitchell's face without him knowing it. Leaning back in his chair, Lawrence takes a pencil from his desk and places the end in his mouth.

"It won't take a minute."

Mitchell looks around the room at the impressive-looking engineering and scientific schematics decorating the walls.

"Impressive." Mitchell nods in recognition.

"A little bit of a scientist too, Agent Mitchell?" Lawrence asks.

"Only in my little bubble of knowledge."

Lawrence perks up. "And what bubble is that?" Lawrence asks.

"Cryptology," Mitchell replies.

"Of course it is: you are NSA. Silly of me, really should have known. The code breakers."

Lawrence seems impressed.

"Are you any good at it?"

A straightforward question deserves a straightforward answer: "Yes, yes I am," Mitchell says confidently. "But to tell you the truth, when I was told CDM stood for Cold Dark Matter, I was none the wiser."

Mitchell does know now. A briefing note from Cameron had been enough to brush up his university lectures on the subject. But Mitchell wants to know how much Lawrence knows, or, more importantly, what Lawrence is willing to tell him.

"Well…" Lawrence is back in play; Mitchell's gambit has paid off. He may get a little bit more out of this meeting than he had first hoped. "Ah, well, put simply," Lawrence continues, "Cold Dark Matter is a term used to describe the missing mass of the universe." Lawrence points to a large picture on the wall that depicts the Milky Way. "Did you know we can only detect about ninety per cent of the matter in the universe, things like our own Milky Way, for example? The space between the stars, galaxies and other universes emits very little radiation, or anything for that matter, to detect it by. This lack of anything acquired the name Cold Dark Matter. We know it exists. Due to the nature of the observable universe, it must. So, several scientific groups set about trying to find it. The CDM project was just one of many working internationally."

Mitchell is looking intently at the picture of the Milky Way on the wall.

"Are you following me so far?" Lawrence adds, rather condescendingly.

"I do have one question. How do you look for something that you can't see and with no detectable emissions?"

"A good question." Lawrence laughs. "This group of scientists searched the heavens for signs of gravity waves emitted from these cold dark areas. General relativity predicts that heavy objects, such as planets, stars, etcetera, that are moving will cause the emission of gravitational waves, ripples in the curvature of space-time. In much the same way as a ship's bow creates a wake as it moves through the ocean. This CDM team was hoping to detect these waves as evidence of the missing mass."

"Did they succeed?" Mitchell asks.

"Inconclusive. The additional outside funding dried up before enough data was accumulated to publish any real evidence."

"I see."

"In fact, interest in the whole idea of CDM has declined considerably since the project's demise. The NSA are the last people I'd have thought would show interest in such an obscure research programme such as this."

"Like I said, it's not so much the project that interests us as the people who were involved in it."

Would it be too impertinent of me to ask why?" Lawrence leans forward in his chair.

"Not in the least. It's simply a routine background check for security passes." Mitchell sounds intentionally unconvincing.

"Hmm, like you said, an exciting life you must lead, Agent Mitchell."

Mitchell snorts a laugh. Miss Bunker enters the room carrying a file.

"Ah, thank you, Miss Bunker."

Placing the file on the desk, she turns and walks back out, closing the door behind her. Mitchell stands.

"Professor, thank you, especially for the science lesson."

Lawrence stands to shake Mitchell's outstretched hand.

"It is my pleasure. Thank you for breaking up what would otherwise be a routine day of paper shuffling. I hope the file will be of help."

Chapter Five

Jo Sands and Hal Cameron are deep in conversation as Mitchell enters Sands' office. Like a scene from a 1930s serial western, both immediately stop talking and watch Mitchell enter and hang up his coat and scarf. His body language is already telling them the answer to the question they had yet to pose.

Mitchell flops defeated into an empty chair.

"Homesick, Mitch?" Cameron offers lightly.

"No need to ask how it went then?" Sands adds.

"I got their file on the CDM project, okay, and I've pulled the last known address of Hunter from it."

"Good, where is he?"

"Carroll County," Mitchell informs them.

"What about Simmons?" Sands asks.

"Nada. Fell off the face of the Earth." Cameron hates to come up empty handed.

"I'm booked on the next flight to Carroll County. Perhaps Hunter will know where she is," Mitchell continues. "I'm sure Lawrence is hiding something from me. Can't put my finger on it, but he knows more than he is letting on. It's like a new coded sequence just popped into the equation. I can see the pattern, but I don't know what the message is. Frustrating as hell."

"But you found Hunter." Sands sounds more positive.

"Karl Hunter seems to have moved out there soon after the CDM project wound down. Living a hermit life, by all accounts, in a remote part of the mountains near St. Lawrence Sound." Mitchell turns to look at Sands directly. "I hope the budget can stretch to it, but I've booked a four-wheel drive vehicle for when I get there. The Storm Prediction Center have put out an advisory of heavy snow in that area."

"I think we could stretch the budget for a Hertz rent-a-car." Sands' smile starts to melt some of Mitchell's frustration away. "Until we can find out what is going on," Sands continues, "we should prepare a safe house for Hunter here in Washington, somewhere close by. We must take seriously the implied threat in Kensington's note, from whomever or whatever 'blank' is."

"I hope he's willing to take the trip with me. I hate sitting next to reluctant passengers on commercial flights." Mitchell looks across at Cameron. "What's the latest on Medvedenko?"

Cameron takes a deep breath and brushes invisible ash from his trousers.

"Our Moscow bureau has just confirmed the earlier Militia report." Cameron takes a long pause. "Medvedenko killed his family, two daughters and his wife, in what they are calling a frenzied attack. And that's a direct quote from the report."

"Sweet Jesus," Sands bursts out, instinctively.

"No motive has been established as to why."

"What, did he just snap?" Sands is grasping to rationalise what she has just heard.

"They don't say," Cameron interjects and continues, "I also managed to get through to the Moscow Academy of Science on the telephone." Cameron looks directly at Mitchell. "And they told me officially and in no uncertain terms that Medvedenko was not attached to them in any way whatsoever—"

Sands cuts Cameron off. "Which is not entirely accurate. Our bureau chief in Moscow believes Medvedenko was on extended medical leave from the Russian Academy and has been for the past few weeks.

"Suffering from what, a mental breakdown?" Mitchell asks.

"They didn't say," Sands replies, a sigh of resignation slips into her voice. "We think they are lying to us," Sands continues.

Cameron smiles broadly at Mitchell, who snorts a giggle as he remembers their earlier talk.

"Kensington's state of health is in question too, right?" Sands concludes.

"Eidelman thought so," Mitchell informs them.

"Coincidence?" both Sands and Cameron chime together.

"To know of someone these days with a mental health issue or a form of depression is commonplace. Mental awareness is progress, as it was never heard of or talked about back in the day," Mitchell adds this observation to the conversation, perhaps to comfort himself rather than the others in the room.

"But two people from the same group so depressed as to take their own lives? What are the chances of that?" Cameron is restless; Mitchell notices for the first time a nicotine patch on Cameron's sleeveless arm.

Sands notices Cameron's agitated state too and throws him a pack of nicotine gum, which he catches, immediately opens and starts chomping. Mitchell is a little surprised that Sands was using the gum too.

"Assuming Kensington and Medvedenko did commit suicide," Sands adds.

"I need more coffee." Mitchell stands and moves to where the coffee table resides. "Anybody else?"

"Yeah, I'll take a cup," Cameron says.

Sands shakes her head: no. Mitchell pours a couple of mugs and hands one to Cameron.

Mitchell continues, "Medvedenko is the key. I'm sure of it. Kensington didn't die alone. His suicide note was taken by someone before Greenbelt PD arrived and it wasn't the *Putzfrau*."

"Cleaning woman, very impressed. Where did you learn German?"

"Mel Brooks' films."

"As far as we can tell," Sands cuts in, "by his own hand. Now Medvedenko is dead, as well as his entire family."

"Massacred, perhaps by him." Cameron sips from his coffee cup. "Two events, only hours apart, linked by CDM."

"Hopefully, Hunter will be able to shed some light on all of this," Cameron adds.

"Which way do you see this one going, Paul?" Sands asks.

Mitchell takes another sip of his coffee and pauses for a moment in thought.

"This is not a cryptology problem. A code exists, and it's tangible, substantial and material in nature. This problem is event-led – a body here, a couple more there. I get the feeling that we came into this thing halfway through. Kensington's death is not the conclusion; Medvedenko's death just proves that. No, this started after the CDM ended. All this, everything occurring now, has something to do with what happened on that project. Perhaps a grudge within the CDM team." Mitchell looks at his watch. "I'd better be going; my flight leaves in an hour."

* * *

The twin prop Islander is only slightly more comfortable than the C130 Mitchell had flown in previously. Thankfully, the flight is short, and Mitchell can see the partially snow-covered runway as the plane approaches.

As the wheels of the Islander touch the tarmac, a swirl of snow blows across Mitchell's window. The roar of the engines in full reverse causes the interior of the Islander to vibrate violently. His body rattles from side to side, as if he were riding the Cyclone Roller Coaster at Coney Island. Mitchell quickly concludes that he really doesn't care for flying that much.

The aircraft taxies to the terminal, a small-bricked building with two glass doors that open onto the runway. As soon as the ground crew waves it to a halt, the aircraft lurches forward on its brakes and stops. Without warning, another ground crew member opens the cabin door and a blast of bitterly cold wind rushes in.

A strong northerly wind slaps Mitchell hard in the face. He moves quickly along with the other three passengers for the shelter of the terminal building.

The freezing wind is no less biting on the street side of the airport. The weather channel report he saw in Washington did forecast it. The Appalachian Mountains are getting a real covering of snow from an artic weather system being dragged down by an unusual pattern of air near the jet stream, so they said.

A GMC Blazer 4x4 is parked just in front of the terminal with his name on a card in the window. Mitchell throws his kit bag into the back and climbs in. The engine roars to life with the turn of a key and the heater is immediately switched to full.

"Homesick for Greenland? My ass!"

* * *

Mitchell brakes and looks at his map. One thing was for certain: hiring the Blazer was perhaps the wisest move he had made in days. The small, narrow, tree-lined mountain track his Magellan GPS had led him to would have been impossible to find in daylight, let alone at night in a snowstorm. The track is now a white path between tall trees. According to the GPS, the cabin Karl Hunter lives in is a few more miles further up the mountain.

Mitchell looks out through the windscreen at the snowstorm surrounding his truck. The visibility is getting worse. To his knowledge, he has no phobias, yet somehow heavy snowfalls make him feel slightly claustrophobic. Despite living in Greenland for the past few years, the feeling has never dissipated. Dense fog is the only other weather phenomena to have a similar effect on him.

"Let's see if there is a weather bulletin on the radio." He is surprised by hearing his own voice and how much it settles him.

After a brief static, probably caused by the storm, he surmises, the radio auto search finds a news station.

"*Taiwanese investors have reacted nervously to news of China's latest muscle-flexing missile test programme and reports of Chinese military manoeuvres near disputed waters off Taiwan. With tensions between the two sides at their highest level in three years, the benchmark TAIEX stock index fell seven per cent before government intervention helped minimise the damage.*"

The differential four-wheel drive carves a path in the snow as it pushes and drags the heavy truck forward. After a short while, peering through the frosted streaks of white left by the undeviating work of the screen wipers, Mitchell can make out a fork in the road ahead, illuminated by the headlights on the front of the truck, yet no road signs are visible from here. He stops the truck at the junction and, zipping his Parker up over his chin, Mitchell gets out.

Walking in front of the truck, using the headlights as a guide, Mitchell wades through the snow to the intersection. On closer inspection, Mitchell can make out a rectangular shape obscured by snow. Using his gloved hand, Mitchell wipes the snow from the shape. He sees a signpost with a burnt mark of an arrow pointing to the left side fork, and carved below the arrow is the legend 'K. Hunter'.

The GMC slides to a stop outside the cabin. Looking through the side window of his truck, Mitchell can see a light emanating from a porch. The light casts a long shadow across a large stack of firewood placed beside the front door.

Zipping his Parker up again, Mitchell gets out of the truck and wades through the drifting snow towards the cabin and the warmth. Through the cold sticky flakes of snow, Mitchell scans the cabin for any sign of life. Out of the corner of his eye, he sees a curtain pulled back and a face appear at the window.

Moments later, the cabin door opens. Mitchell stumbles in and the door is closed behind him.

"Thanks."

Mitchell turns to see who has opened the door. Unzipping his coat and shaking loose snow from his fringe, Mitchell is surprised to see a young-looking woman standing by the door. The woman looks no more than twenty-five years old, with shoulder length blonde hair. He can't help but notice that she is very pretty.

"This is a hard place to find, especially in this weather."

Mitchell stamps his feet and snow and slush create a puddle on the floor where he is standing.

"Oh, sorry about that." Mitchell looks apologetically at the water on the rug.

"That's okay." The woman takes a roll of kitchen paper from the nearby breakfast bar, pulls off three sheets and hands it to Mitchell.

"Thanks. I'm Paul Mitchell from the National Security Agency."

Mitchell fumbles to retrieve his identification from his pocket while holding the wet tissue paper.

"NSA? You want me?"

"If you are Karl Hunter I do, but somehow, I don't think you are. Am I in the right place?"

The woman moves away from the door into the living area, where a raging fire is blazing in the hearth. Mitchell assumes her moving into the warmth of the living room is an invitation for him to loosen his coat and join her. Mitchell takes off his Parker. As more snow falls onto the rug, he just leaves his coat in a pile on the already soaked carpet.

"Yes, you are. The cheating bastard you were looking for lives here. Well, he did. He moved out around the end of November, three, four weeks back."

Seeing the woman's face more clearly now, Mitchell can see she is fighting back tears.

"I'm sorry, and you are?"

"Rachel, Rachel Simmons."

Mitchell is momentarily taken aback.

"Rachel Simmons? You worked with Karl on CDM project too, right?"

"As well as others, yes. I was a team leader along with Karl, John and Anton." She continues, "Until the funding dried up."

"And you and Karl stayed in touch?"

"We were lovers then. 'Were' being the operative word. John Kensington introduced us when he put his team together and, well, we just hit it off immediately."

"Where is Karl now?"

"He said I could stay here and get my shit together for as long as I liked. Considerate of him, don't you think? Makes a girl fall in love with him and then lets you stay in his mountain retreat to get over him. A real Don Juan that man."

"He's gone then?"

"Yep. We stayed together for almost six years, after the project closed. He just wandered off to pastures new and green." She laughs out loudly and points outside to the snow falling. "Let me tell you, that bastard changed after CDM closed down."

For the first time, Mitchell realises Simmons is slightly drunk.

"He was so damn snappy too! I couldn't do a thing right. And jealous, Jesus," she continues. "I couldn't even talk to a colleague on the phone without him accusing me of having an affair. No, sir. He wasn't the happy-go-lightly whiz kid I fell in love with. After about a year of arguing we drifted apart, coming to a head, I guess, three to four weeks ago when he split. And he went off on some damn long research trip on board the *Aurora*."

"The *Aurora*?" Mitchell asks.

"Yeah, she's an Antarctic research ship, currently roaming the southern hemisphere for a couple of years monitoring the hole in the ozone. Funded by Greenpeace, totally independent, that's why you won't find the expedition on any scientific records."

Simmons flops on to a comfortable sofa near the fire and reaches out for a glass of white wine on a side table. She takes a long drink from the glass.

"I'm sorry, would you care for some? The bastard's got a great cellar."

"Why not." Mitchell takes a seat opposite Simmons, while she pours another glass. She holds her arm outstretched for him to take it. Shuffling forward on the sofa, Mitchell takes the glass.

"Thank you."

"So, Agent Mitchell."

"Please, call me Paul."

"Okay, Paul, how can I help you?" Simmons snuggles down on the sofa and as she settles, takes another sip of wine.

"I had in mind to talk to Karl about CDM, specifically about John Kensington. But now you're here, I am—"

"John? Now, he is a nice man. His wife left him, you know, after he left CDM – second time, too, since the end of CDM. No more regular hours, I guess. John was back to the irregular astronomy timetables and assignments."

A deep sigh and a stare into the embers of the fire in the hearth. She is much slower in her speech now.

"Radio telescope work is the worst because those babies are plugged in 24/7. You don't have to have it dark with radio astronomy. Because of that, they are booked up by teams, from across the world, every single day of the year, years in advance, for their projects to get time on them."

Simmons takes another long sip of wine.

"You know a lot about astronomy etiquette."

"It's the rules of the game. You must join the queue, like everyone else, to get your go playing with the big boy toys. Amazing, isn't it? You get nice men like John, a dedicated man, devoted to his family, lovely kids and a wife who likes her husband around more. Well, what do you expect when you marry an astronomer? The sky is 24/7 too, for Christ's sake."

Mitchell notices her speech is getting slightly more slurred. It is incredibly cute though, he thinks. She takes another sip of wine.

"I haven't seen John since leaving the CDM project; Christ, that must have been five or six years ago now. I tried calling him a few times, especially since the bastard left me, but I guess he was busy, as I never heard back from him."

"Perhaps you could help," Mitchell says between sips of his wine. "Was there any animosity between Kensington and any of the other CDM members?"

"Animosity, against John? Hell no, lovely man. Well respected by us all and he saw to it we all had good jobs to go to after CDM was shut down."

"You said you haven't seen Kensington since the end of CDM."

Simmons pours herself another glass of wine as she talks. "That's right."

"What about letters, emails, any correspondence?"

"Not for years, none."

Mitchell is curious; what about the suicide note?

"The only one I kept in touch with was the bastard."

Simmons, despite the wine, is getting wise to the fact that there is more to Mitchell's questions than at first meets the eye.

"What's going on? Why all the questions about a defunct project six years out of date?"

"Well." Mitchell knows the pleasantries can't last much longer; He pauses to allow himself a moment to select the right words. "There is no real easy way of saying this, so, John Kensington and Anton Medvedenko are both dead."

Mitchell shuffles forward on his seat to be closer to Simmons. Her face immediately turns red, and her eyes once again begin to water.

"Dead?" Her voice is weak.

"Yes." Mitchell is concerned; he should have told her later. *She is in no fit state to hear this news*, he thinks, but it is too late now.

"I'm sorry," Mitchell speaks softly, "I was hoping Karl Hunter could give us some help in trying to understand all this?"

"What happened? An accident, but how? Why? What happened?"

"They didn't die together, but—"

Simmons interrupts, "But you said they were both dead."

"They were not together; Medvedenko was home in Russia and Kensington died in Maryland. We're not sure what happened but their deaths are being investigated."

"Who is investigating?" Simmons asks. Rage slowly rises in her voice now.

"Me." Mitchell looks resolute. "What we have is just pure speculation at this moment. It appears both men had been suffering from depression."

Mitchell looks into his wine glass to allow Simmons a moment of private grief as the tears roll down her face.

"Their poor families. I know things had been difficult between John and Beverley, but Anton adored his wife and kids. They were his pride and joy. He carried a picture of them in his wallet and showed it to anyone who would stand still long enough. They will be devastated." Simmons wipes her face on the sleeve of her jumper.

Mitchell isn't about to make the same mistake twice; she doesn't need to know about Medvedenko's family or the way they were found.

"The thing is," Mitchell continues, "their deaths occurred close enough together in a timeline of events that it makes coincidence an outside bet. We must be cautious here and we are concerned about the rest of the CDM team's well-being."

"Could I be in danger too?" Simmons clasps a fist full of jumper over her breast, near her heart.

"It's a possibility," Mitchell calmly adds. "We found what could be a suicide note in Kensington's home."

"A note?"

"Yes." Mitchell stands and retrieves his Parka from the floor where he dumped it on arrival. He reaches into an inner coat pocket and takes out a slip of paper. "The note was headed to 'R'."

"I see."

He looks at it before reading it to Simmons.

"May I read it to you?"

Simmons nods yes in agreement.

"*R*

"*Can't tinue. o much pr es knows I need to tal . I*

"*you'll understand.*

"*I'll be ing for you the othersi Be areful e may*

"*after all us John.*"

Mitchell continues, "Most of the letters are missing. We don't have the original. This is a copy I made from the desk protector," Mitchell explains. "'R' could be mean you, 'R' for Rachel, I guess, but you say you've had no correspondence with Kensington for a number of years."

"That's right. The first time Karl and I separated. I spoke to John then. He was very sympathetic. He explained that Karl's ego gets the better of him at times, and he would come back once his ego gets buried in his work."

"I see."

"In the note, Kensington says he needs to talk. Do you know what that would be about?"

"To me? No." It is obvious to Mitchell that Simmons is trying her hardest to sober up and be of help.

Also, this concern John has that someone is after you all, this blank here," Mitchell points to the copy of the note, "he does not want you to speak to him. You have no idea who that could be?"

"No. He obviously feels threatened."

"Strange, isn't it? If you are the 'R' in the note, it gives the impression that he's kept in contact with you since Karl left for the first time, at least. People who haven't seen each other in a while aren't usually as familiar as this note suggests."

"If it's true what you say about John, perhaps he was under a lot of mental stress. Who knows what was going through his mind? I know that your sense of time can be distorted when you're under emotional pressure. That's one of the reasons I escaped the city and came up here after Karl left; there's very little stress here." Simmons sits up.

"Still, it is odd. Why do you think, after an absence of contact for a few years, he would address his last thoughts to you?"

Simmons is silent. Mitchell takes the copy of the note from Simmons' hand.

"Odd," Simmons finally offers.

"You'll have to come back to Washington with me, Miss Simmons."

She is stunned by his comment. "Surely I'm not under arrest?"

"No, no. Of course not. The fact is we have two deaths that are linked to a science project you worked on. If the threats mentioned in this note are real, we need to protect you and Dr. Hunter, and for that we need you back in Washington, D.C."

"Wow. Are you sure that is necessary?"

"I'm afraid so." Mitchell looks at his wristwatch.

"Just collect a few things together. We haven't much time as I've reserved two seats on the next flight to Dulles."

"Jesus, you don't hang about, do you? Very well, I'll pack a bag."

Simmons downs the last drop of wine from her glass and winces slightly as the gooseberry and citrus flavours of the wine catch in her throat.

"Gah!" she exclaims. "Fifteen minutes tops."

"Sounds good," Mitchell approves of her time frame.

While Simmons moves, slightly wobbly on her legs, towards what he assumes is the bedroom, Mitchell moves to the fire and begins to break up the embers, extinguishing the flames. Soon the fire is nothing more than smouldering charcoal. Mitchell crosses the room and looks out of the window at the blizzard raging outside.

"We'd best hurry; the weather is closing in on us."

Simmons' soft voice replies from the adjacent room, as Mitchell puts on his outdoor coat, "How long do you think I'll have to stay in Washington?"

"Until we are sure you're no longer in any danger. Don't worry about taking too little. You can pick up more clothes when you get to Washington. The NSA will pick up the tab."

Mitchell turns from the window and walks over to the fireplace again to check it for the last time. Mitchell looks up at the personal pictures displayed on the mantelshelf. His gaze stops on a picture of Dr. Karl Hunter standing outside the cabin in another snowy scene, holding a string of wild wood pigeons, smiling into the camera. He is a very 'Hollywood' handsome man; you can see why Simmons fell for him.

"These pictures above the fire – how long ago were these taken?"

Simmons enters the room carrying a large sports bag. Over her jumper, she has put on a padded, green, quilted jacket. Mitchell likes the look. She walks over to the fireplace and looks at the photographs with him.

"When I first moved in. I find it hard to believe I've lived anywhere else. This is where my home is now."

"It must get pretty lonely up here."

"Sometimes."

Mitchell takes her bag.

"If I remember correctly, living in the city isn't a guarantee of not being lonely either," Simmons says, coyly.

"That's so true."

They both turn to leave. Simmons looks to check the guard around the open fire and then switches off the living room lights. As Mitchell opens the front door, a gust of cold air and snow rushes into the room. Simmons walks out through the door first and Mitchell closes the door and moves to one side, as Simmons fumbles, with her gloved hands, for the keys to lock the door.

Mitchell walks towards his parked jeep, keys ready, intending to get the engine on and the heater warmed up. Mitchell notices that the car has acquired a good two inches of snow on its roof since he pulled up. The wind is beginning to howl through the nearby trees, as snow turns into a blizzard, reducing visibility further. Mitchell puts Simmons' sports bag onto the back seat and turns to look back at the cabin, where she is fumbling at the door.

"Come on! This is getting bad! I hope the track down from here is clear, otherwise we'll never get off this mountain in time for the flight!"

Simmons turns to look at Mitchell, then turns back to the frozen lock on her front door. Mitchell starts to clear the heavy snow off the windscreen with his forearm. Finally, the door locks and Simmons turns to join Mitchell in the car. Mitchell turns to see her progress and smiles as she holds her arms above her head in triumph, as if she has just won the one-hundred-metre dash.

Suddenly, from out of the trees a burst of gunfire rains across the porch. Two bullets explode into Simmons' chest, and she is violently flung backwards against the cabin door. Mitchell dives for cover behind his car and quickly looks to the motionless body of Rachel Simmons.

His mouth is agape. His eyes are wide open in shock. Even in the whiteout of the blizzard, Mitchell can see blood seeping from the sides of her mouth. Where once a fog of frozen air would linger by her nose and mouth, there is now nothing.

She is dead.

* * *

Mitchell spins around on his knees and aims his sidearm at the tree line. As suddenly as before, a fierce volley of gunfire peppers the side of Mitchell's car, forcing Mitchell back to the ground for what little cover he can find.

Mitchell looks over to where Simmons lies – not a movement. Another hail of bullets rips into the GMC, shattering the glass in the side door and the windscreen. As the bullets tear into the jeep, Mitchell looks round the front tyre, into the tree line, spotting the fire flash from the automatic weapon and, without hesitation, he returns rapid fire.

The assassin returns fire, forcing Mitchell to dig deep into the snow-covered ground. Shattered glass from the GMC showers down on top of him like frozen rain. More bullets bombard the jeep's chassis, as Mitchell reloads his .45 blindly, arms held out flat, keeping as low a profile as possible. As suddenly as the shooting started, it stops.

The silence now only amplifies the ringing Mitchell has in his ears from the hail of bullets. Thankfully, his ears are the only things hurting. He is not hit. Mitchell opens the side door of the jeep. He climbs up, over the spider's web of shattered windscreen that now occupies the front of his car, into the driver's seat. The shattered windscreen now gives no protection from the driving snow outside and the interior of the jeep is already filling up with snow. Mitchell starts the engine and selects drive. Keeping his head down and recalling the position of the jeep where he parked it first, he turns the steering wheel of the jeep towards the tree line and, using his hand on the accelerator pedal, drives towards the gunman.

As he expected, the assassin is not gone, just reloading, as a cascade of bullets slices into the front of the jeep. The jeep now reaches twenty miles an hour, as its full force and weight crashes through the young trees on the edge of the covering, breaking a path to where the gunman is hiding.

Each tree encountered jolts the jeep back on its suspension. The bigger trees make the engine roar, as the wheels are lifted momentarily from the path. Inside the jeep, glass and snow continue to rain down over Mitchell.

The jeep abruptly stops. A tree branch thrusts itself through the open windscreen and spears the headrest of the passenger seat. The engine roars at high revolutions, as Mitchell is thrown to the floor.

Mitchell reaches up, switching the engine off. Silence falls. Another engine, not too far away starts up. Scrambling up from the floor of the jeep, Mitchell catches his coat on the branch of the tree above him. Ripping his coat free, he slides into the driving seat and tries to restart the jeep's engine. The starter motor clicks over, but the engine fails to fire.

"Come on! Come on!"

The engine roars into life and Mitchell puts it into reverse. The branch and some of the headrest pull free of the jeep.

Following the path he made through the trees, Mitchell soon arrives back outside the house. Simmons' body is illuminated by the porch light. Simmons' body is motionless, still lying where she was shot, light snow collecting on her face and coat.

Spinning the jeep in the snow, he faces down the mountain track and accelerates away. It is not long before the brake lights of the vehicle in front can been seen. The red glow pierces the white haze of the snowstorm. The assassin's car is no match for the four-wheel drive of the GMC Jeep, and it slides from side to side down the snow-packed mountain track. The powerful jeep is soon bumper to bumper with the assassin and, for the first time in this encounter, Mitchell has the upper hand. He rams the rear of the car, forcing it to take even more erratic evasive action.

Mitchell rams it again, this time pushing it down the track in front of him.

"Come on, you bastard."

Mitchell senses blood in his nose and mouth as his rage, adrenaline and fear rise inside him.

The end of the track nears as the valley road approaches and tarmac appears fleetingly on the path ahead. Feeling the jeep gain more traction, Mitchell takes aim with his pistol firing three rounds into the back of the assassin' car, smashing the rear glass, as both cars veer onto the road.

A snow plough is in the middle of the road, making both cars brake and slide. The snow plough driver immediately turns to avoid the assassin's car, which bounces off the snow plough and passes down one side. The jeep slides into the path of the snow plough and skids to a halt in front of it. The bright yellow truck rams the jeep, knocking it on its side, pushing it along the road for a few feet, before it finally stops.

Mitchell lays semi-conscious inside the jeep as the assassin escapes down the valley road.

* * *

Mitchell stands at a pay phone, the receiver balanced between his right ear and his shoulder. He taps the last number in. Mitchell is bruised and bloody but alive. The hospital corridor is warm, but the emergency room exterior door is constantly opening and closing, and the emergency staff all wear heavy coats to keep the chilly wind out. The sterile strips over his left eye and right cheek make his face feel taught like a poor man's Botox treatment. Mitchell rubs his swollen eye. After a short while, the phone connects.

"Sands speaking."

"Jo? It's Paul." On hearing Jo's voice for the first time since Simmons' murder, he feels emotional.

"Where are you?" Sands is surprised to hear his voice.

"In a hospital lobby near St. Lawrence, I don't know which one. Apparently, I've been unconscious for a couple of hours."

Mitchell shuffles his feet, uncomfortable with the words forming in his mouth.

"Rachel Simmons is dead."

"What?" A nurse passing Mitchell hears Sands' question.

"Listen, I'm on a pay phone, but the local cops have her body now. Check it out with them. I found Simmons in Karl Hunter's cabin. They were partners, lovers, until last November. That's when she said they split. He left her and he joined a research ship, sailing in the south Atlantic."

Mitchell takes a deep breath. It hurt doing so.

"It was a professional hit, Jo. Rachel didn't have a chance. The bastards were waiting for us right outside Hunter's cabin. There wasn't anything I could do."

Mitchell winces with pain as his back twinges.

"I got hurt chasing them." He pauses momentarily, more due to his embarrassment at his failure, than the pain from his injuries. "They got away."

"Are you fit enough to travel?"

"Yeah, I suppose so. Everything okay your end?" Mitchell is a little puzzled.

"I want you to come back to Washington, immediately."

"What the hell for? Simmons was killed here; I can't do a damn thing in Washington!"

"Paul, we're off the case."

"What?"

"It's been turned over to the FBI."

"They don't have any jurisdiction on this case."

“The State Department believes that there’s not enough evidence of a national security threat to warrant any further NSA involvement.”

“So, some field agent out here is going to investigate Simmons’ murder?” Mitchell is fuming. “I was almost killed too, Jo, how much fucking evidence do they want?”

“I quote from the memo I got: ‘The case doesn’t involve any current high-level personnel, nor is of national importance.’.”

Mitchell is thinking on his feet, despite the monumental headache that feels like the two halves of his brain are being squeezed together.

“I’ll have to stay here anyway. The FBI will want to ask me questions,” is the only feeble excuse he can muster.

“If they want you, they can reach you here,” Sands informs Mitchell officially.

Mitchell is fast getting the impression that Sands has had enough of this conversation.

“Now get your ass on a plane back here now!”

Mitchell slams the receiver of the pay phone down.

“Fuck!”

* * *

The dialling tone can be heard as Sands slowly puts the phone down. Sands glances across the room. Her room is dark; the blinds are closed, and her desk lamp is the only light on. She sighs deeply.

“Okay?”

A figure sits in the darkness of the room. A plume of white smoke soon engulfs a bright red glow from a large cigar being drawn upon. Ash from the cigar falls onto one of their shoes. He leans forward slowly and brushes the grey ash from his highly polished, stylised, patent leather shoes.

“Yes, Miss Sands.”

* * *

Mitchell walks through the outer offices of the Washington Bureau of the NSA. His injuries are still apparent on his face, but by now he has grown accustomed to staring. A pair of sunglasses conceals most of the cuts and bruises on his face. Mitchell strides purposefully to Sands' office, ignoring friendly enquiries from colleagues as to his injuries. Sands' office door is open and, without knocking, he enters. Sands is sitting behind her desk.

"Jesus, Paul, you arsehole! You scared the life out of me!" She grabs her chest in a simulated heart attack. Her blouse is pushed to one side, revealing her bra. Despite Mitchell's much-rehearsed tirade, he is caught off guard by her indiscretion.

Sands, unknowingly, has defused the bomb.

"Come in and close the door," Sands says, calmly.

Mitchell enters the room fully now and closes the door. Sands readjusts her blouse and motions for Mitchell to take a seat.

"First, let me say I'm sorry about what happened, especially to you. I hate all of this just as much as you, being told what to do by faceless bureaucrats in the State Department. But my hands were tied – I'm sorry."

Mitchell senses she is sincere. Nevertheless, he rehearsed what he is going to say on the flight back to D.C., and he isn't about to waste all of that preparation.

"Don't give me all that. You weren't there. It was like a damn turkey shoot!

"Listen, I understand all of that."

"Well, I don't! What's all this about no justification to warrant an NSA investigation? I've been on this one from the outset. The NSA works hand in hand with the scientific community, not the FBI."

Mitchell's anger is false. He knows Sands wants to find out what the hell is going on just as much as he does, but for Christ's sake, he reasons, "I was shot at!"

"As I have said to you on the phone," Sands speaks calmly, "this matter has been re-classified and no longer qualifies as an NSA case, regardless of any Grizzly Adams taking pot shots at you."

She looks down at her desk, not able to look Mitchell in the eye.

"I'm sorry. The FBI will find Simmons' killer and that's the end of it as far as we are concerned."

"Bullshit! You can't just pull me off the case because it's not in line with departmental policy."

Sands looks up.

Mitchell continues, "If you don't back up your field agents when they need it, then what good are you?"

Sands is visibly hurt by the remark. Mitchell knows just where to hit. There is a history between them and knowing where your hypothetical blows do the most damage is a byproduct of a failed relationship. Mitchell knows Sands hates to feel useless.

"How dare you lecture me. I was in the field for three years before—"

"Three years? I've been a field operative for fifteen years," Mitchell snaps back.

"Yeah right, and what does that tell you?"

Mitchell places both of his clenched fists on Sands' desk and glares directly into her eyes.

"It tells me," he says, punching home each point, "that good legs and great tits means more than fifteen years of experience to get ahead."

Mitchell turns and leaves Sands' office, wrenching open the door so that it crashes into the furniture behind it. He walks out without turning back.

"I want all your paperwork handed in to the bureau, today!" she shouts after him.

Mitchell continues to walk down the corridor without looking back. He feels bad. Sands is a good friend and he hurt her, but he can't take back what he said. He needs a drink.

* * *

Mitchell sits at the bar, drinking a beer with a whiskey chaser, a drink his father had introduced him to as a surly youth. His dad taught him many things, including how to drink. His wise words are still with Mitchell, all these years later. "*When you have had a rough day, don't drink to be happy. Alcohol doesn't work that way. It's fine to drink when you are happy. The drink you need on a bad day is called a Boilermaker.*" And that is the perfect drink for the day he was having.

In the parlance of the D.C. district, he was drinking in an old hangout for off-duty and retired police officers of mainly Irish decent. The obligatory TV is above the bar counter and, like a few others nearby, he watches the news.

"*The Gaza Strip is once again a hotspot of violence and turmoil post the 7 October raid by Hamas.*"

"Turn it off, will ya, Murray? Put the fecking game back on!" a patron calls out to the bar keeper, who casually flicks the remote over to the NFL channel. A cheer fills the bar.

The bar is surprisingly busy for the time of day and there is a buzz in the air to match that currently in Mitchell's head.

Hal Cameron enters and is surprised by the smoke-filled bar. Seeing Mitchell, he heads over and plants himself down on the empty barstool next to him. Mitchell looks across at Cameron, raises his glass and downs another shot.

"Hell of a day, huh?" Cameron surmises.

"Another shot here please, Pat." Mitchell indicates his empty glass to the bartender. "You could say that."

"What the hell did you say to Jo, anyway? She's been biting people's heads off since you left."

"Too much." Mitchell is melancholy. He continues, "It's getting so that you can't even complement a colleague on their physical attributes anymore without consequences. Want a beer?"

Cameron looks at his watch, puzzled.

"Sure, let's call it an early brunch, why not?"

Mitchell signals the bartender for two more beers. Cameron notices for the first time that Mitchell is a little drunk.

"How long have you been here?" Cameron sets his cigarettes on the counter.

"Long enough to think things through."

The bartender arrives with their beers and one whiskey chaser.

Mitchell collects both of his drinks and motions Cameron to follow him to an empty booth. Cameron collects his things and follows. They sit down, placing their drinks in front of them.

"Sands seems to think this CDM thing isn't a concern for us anymore."

"I know."

"Well, she's wrong."

Mitchell takes a sip from his beer.

"What's the latest on the FBI's investigation into Simmons' assassination?"

Cameron is stunned. "Assassination? That's not what the Feds are telling us. Sands has given authorisation that all your files are to be taken over to the Hoover Building. She's not a very happy bunny, let me tell you, but she's playing along. I suppose she hasn't much choice."

"There are always options, Hal."

"Are you considering yours?"

"I'm not going to resign, if that's what you mean." Mitchell investigates Cameron's face for a reaction. "Unless, of course, I've already been fired?"

"Not even Sands would allow that to happen."

"Don't underestimate her. I was angry earlier and said some things."

"Come on, Paul. She's tough." For the first time, Cameron realises what a state his friend is in. "Jesus, look at your face!"

"You should see the other guy," Mitchell exclaims.

"Not a scratch on them. Am I right, huh?"

"Clean as a whistle."

They both laugh.

"I guess I thought I'd get a more sympathetic hearing than I did from Jo."

"I only hope you got information or something from Simmons that makes all of this worth it."

"It's more what I didn't get from her."

"You're babbling, Paul. What are you talking about? What about the note?"

"When I showed her my copy, she looked genuinely shocked by it. And she couldn't fill in the blank name either."

"She could just be a good actress, Mitch."

"We're so close to finding out what is going on I can almost taste it, Hal. The Feds will drag their feet, as usual."

"It doesn't matter how long they take. It's out of our hands now.

Mitchell turns to look at Cameron.

"We got close to the truth. Finding Simmons in Hunter's cabin was a bit of luck, I grant you. She got killed for talking to me and she is dead now. By the time the FBI have figured all that out, the trail will be as cold as a witch's tit."

"So, what are you saying? What are you going to do?" Cameron is concerned.

"I've been through the mill a few times since I started this case; too many people don't want me to finish. And I don't know why. I just can't drop now, Hal, not now. The solution lies with the surviving CDM team members and I'm going to find out what this shit is all about."

"How? If Sands finds out you're still working on it, she'll drop a bomb from low earth orbit on you!"

"I can't use the agency's resources for a start. That's obvious."

"You must be kidding. It will take you forever to track people, documents, emails or gain access to government files without the agency." Cameron lights a cigarette. "Let alone the use of the labs," he adds, through a plume of smoke.

Mitchell smiles. "What about Hawks?"

"Hawks?" Cameron splutters in disbelief. "Alvin Hawks is not the most reliable of people. His prison record speaks for that."

"He may not be reliable but he's trustworthy."

"As a pin prick tester in a condom factory," Cameron snaps back.

"I'd keep an eye on him," Mitchell says.

"I'd use both of them if I were you."

"I don't know of anyone better qualified at getting into highly classified computer systems than Hawks, do you?"

Cameron thinks silently for a moment. "No, I guess not. He certainly knows the NSA computers systems well enough; he's hacked into them enough times."

Cameron's tone is almost appreciative towards Hawks' skills.

"I'm hoping he can do the same thing with the FBI systems." Mitchell smiles.

"You know if he gets caught, he will have no compunction

to blab as fast as his jaw muscles will allow. It will mean the end of your career, Paul – you'll be kicked out of the agency, loss of pension, everything at best. At worst, Kansas will be your home for many years to come."

"Kansas?" Mitchell doesn't follow.

"Leavenworth Maximum Security Prison is in Kansas, my friend. There's no place like home, there's no place like home."

"Idiot." Mitchell holds back a smile. "He won't get caught. He could run rings round those goons."

Mitchell feels better. He now has a plan, of sorts, and sitting in a bar is not part of it. He downs the last dregs of his beer.

"I guess I should get back to the office and play nice with Sands," Mitchell says, shrugging his shoulders.

"I think that would be a good idea, for all of us who have to work in the same building as her."

"Yeah, I'm sure the whole department would appreciate it."

Mitchell smiles in agreement.

* * *

Mitchell and Cameron walk through the outer offices of the NSA building, attracting as much attention as if they were naked and painted bright green. Agents and auxiliary staff alike stop in mid flow of what they are doing and follow the two men with their gaze.

It is common knowledge that Sands' wrath, when exposed to light, is legendary. It is a combination of being explosive, articulate and yet funny, especially funny, if you were not on the receiving end it.

The two men quickly sense they are the centre of attention. To make matters worse, like two gladiators entering the Colosseum to fight to the death, someone starts to slow clap them. Soon the clapping increases, punctuated by catcalls and whistles. Without signalling to each other, both men clench their fists, hit their chests, and do a Roman salute, which is rewarded by a loud cheer.

Mitchell smiles broadly. A young messenger, reluctant to get involved, thrusts a message into Mitchell's hand. He quickly stops to reads it.

"Bad news?" Cameron asks.

"Sands wants to meet me over at State, immediately."

"You mean we went through all this for nothing? She give a reason?"

"Nope, but I bet it's not to discuss seating arrangements at her Christmas dinner table."

Mitchell pulls Cameron to one side as the office returns to relative normality.

"Do me favour, will you? Copy every file I have on this case and hide it somewhere."

"If they're still here, sure, but where do you want me to hide them?

"Create a file, a 'John Doe' file or something, but hide it."

"Okay."

Mitchell turns and walks to the elevator.

"I'll call you when I get back."

* * *

The taxi turns right off Constitution Avenue onto Virginia Avenue and enters Edward J Kelly Park en route to the State Department building main entrance. Mitchell likes D.C. parks, and this one looks particularly lovely today, covered in a blanket of snow. But like most D.C. dwellers he knows taxi rides are not the best way to see the city, as with most D.C. taxi drivers, there is an unknown urgency about the ride that makes passengers far too cautious to relax and enjoy the view, knowing that, at any moment, they could be scraping themselves off the floor of the cab.

The cab pulls up smartly outside the main entrance to what, in effect, is the main portal to and from the United States. The State Department issues passports and visas, assigns diplomats to embassies across the globe, and dictates foreign policy.

Mitchell wonders why Sands is here. By the time Mitchell has buttoned his coat, the taxi has gone, no doubt racing another unsuspecting tourist or D.C. dweller on a lightning-fast ride though the city. The steps to the main entrance had been cleared of snow and light brown grit crunches under his feet as he jogs up the steps.

Mitchell presents his credentials at reception to the uniformed Customs and Immigration officer. It is a well-known and documented fact that the US Customs and Immigration Service, which is without question the most officious bunch of Dudley Do-Rights within the US Civil Service system, are perhaps the most humourless and gruff uniformed body in the world, except for airport customs officers, of course.

It seems to them that everyone they ever encounter is an alien invader, intent on stealing their children for food. Mitchell had expected nothing better than he gets, which is stony silence, while his ID is scrutinised.

Without even an acknowledgement of his existence, the desk officer hands Mitchell his ID back and signals another officer to the desk. Handing a piece of paper to the escort, Mitchell is dismissed by a nod of the head and the next unfortunate citizen is ushered forward for processing.

Silently, Mitchell mouths the word, "Charming."

In silence, Mitchell is escorted through the building and eventually they arrive at a double oak-panelled door.

"Agent Mitchell, they are expecting you inside."

They speak! Mitchell was beginning to wonder if anyone from the US State Department could. Mitchell knocks and walks in.

The wood-panelled room is richly decorated with historical portraits, mainly of American ambassadors, and tall dressers, packed full of fine china and glassware from England, Japan, and Russia. Jo Sands is seated on a leather couch in the far corner of the room. Mitchell smiles apologetically and shrugs his shoulders, but Sands' face is sombre and pensive.

"Jo, I'm sorry about what I said earlier. You know I didn't mean any of it—" Mitchell is cut off in mid-sentence.

"You had better close the door, Agent Mitchell."

Mitchell turns and sees an elderly man seated behind a large oak desk. He speaks calmly and with authority. Another man moves from the shadows of a bookcase and stands by the desk. He rests his fingers on some files, as if trying to stop a breeze from blowing them away. Both look very serious.

Mitchell closes the door. A third man appears from an adjacent room; he enters and silently closes the connecting door behind him. Mitchell looks curiously at him, then turns to look at Sands. Sands beckons him to sit next to her and Mitchell quickly seats himself.

"These gentlemen are from the State Department, Paul. They've invited us here to ensure a clean handover to the Bureau of the Kensington case." Sands brings Mitchell up to speed.

"That's right, Agent Mitchell," the standing man speaks, making Mitchell turn from looking at Sands. "We want to help clear up any misunderstandings you may have and to ensure that the FBI have your total co-operation and that of Ms. Sands' department."

"I can assure you, gentlemen," Sands is speaking with her telephone voice, "of my department's full co-operation."

Sands places her hand on Mitchell's knee and squeezes it – painfully.

"And as for Agent Mitchell, I can—"

"Speak for myself." Mitchell takes Sands' hand away. Mitchell glances at Sands. "Excuse my ignorance here, but why is the State Department having to be in the FBI's corner over this little misunderstanding, as you call it?"

Another new voice joins in, not as high as the last speaker's voice, but dry. The voice comes from the last man to enter the room.

"Standard operating procedure, that is all, Agent Mitchell."

The man now walks to a small round table and, sitting on the edge, he folds his arms. The muscles beneath his suit make the sleeves of his jacket tight. After a closer look, Mitchell isn't entirely convinced this man has sat behind a desk all his working life. Lifted a few, maybe.

The seated desk man continues, "A material witness to a murder cannot be party to the ensuing investigation. You know that."

"You're talking about Simmons?" Mitchell enquires.

"Of course," the man standing at the desk now speaks. "Your inquiries into this matter ended with her death."

Mitchell whispers to Sands, "Nice and convenient."

"And as for your notes and files, Agent Mitchell," Mr. Gravelly voice contributes his nickel's worth from behind the desk, "the Bureau are already on their way to your office to collect your files so that we can proceed without hesitation or interruption."

"Is that right?" Mitchell knows as soon as the words leave his mouth that there is an edge to them. "So, tell me again, what has this got to do with State?" Mitchell asks.

"Who said it did?" Muscles replied.

"Well, I assumed that because I was summoned here by you and that we are now having this conversation inside one of their offices—"

The man standing by the desk interrupts, "There are many federal agencies involved now, Agent Mitchell, from the local law enforcement office in St. Lawrence to State Police and now the FBI."

Muscles pipes in again, "Of course, we are also interested in any insights you may have on the case. Your thoughts, your instincts, things that wouldn't necessarily be in your files."

Mitchell knows the law well enough. What these men are telling him is technically correct, but what his instincts were telling him is something else. This is not the entire story. He is being pushed into a corner and it is time to push back.

"My instinct? My instinct tells me I'll have to wait a good few more years before I hear this much bullshit spoken in one room again."

Sands elbows Mitchell hard in the ribs. It hurts.

* * *

The wood-panelled door closed quickly behind them, leaving Sands and Mitchell alone in the corridor. Mitchell led the way to the elevator, rubbing his ribs.

"What the fuck was that for?" Mitchell was not naturally foul-mouthed, openly. It sounded wrong every time he spoke that way.

"Sorry, I forgot you were in an accident."

"Yeah, my face looks like this most of the time." Sarcasm is much more his style.

"Not a bad punch for nothing more than a collection of tits and legs then?"

They reach the elevators and Mitchell laughs as he presses the down button.

"Yeah, I'm sorry about that. You still mad?"

"Damn right I'm mad!"

The elevator doors open, and they step inside the empty elevator car. Mitchell waits until the doors are closed and they are alone before he asks the question.

"What the hell is going on, Jo?"

"I don't know, something isn't right for sure, but this is one puzzle we will have to live with unsolved, okay?"

Sands is rattled, Mitchell could tell.

"Besides, this business in Israel requires all NSA agents to be on their toes – you know how quickly these things escalate?"

"So, I just jump back on a plane and head home to my little igloo at the North Pole, is that it?"

"Don't get any ideas about sticking your nose back into this one, Paul. I told you I had a bad feeling about it from the start. It's over, I mean it, okay?"

"Nag, nag, nag."

* * *

Every employee of the National Security Agency from the newest receptionist to the director of operations has a unique five-digit passcode that records their every move inside NSA buildings nationwide. That means every room they enter or file they take must be recorded via their unique code.

The same goes for the photocopying machines. The system is foolproof, unless you are Hal Cameron, who, many years ago, had a high school friend who now is the chief designer at Cobra Security. The company, which manufactures and supplies all government security systems, made Hal, his NSA friend, a digital skeleton passcode key. A preset passcode, used by system maintenance engineers, that is totally unrecorded.

Despite being 'invisible' to the system, Cameron works hurriedly, copying the Kensington files. It would have been easier to download the files and hide them, but computers are not as secure as anti-spyware manufactures would have you believe. Hard copies can be put in a shoebox under a bed anywhere in the world and there is no computer hacker capable of finding those files – yet.

Cameron watches the copied files emerge from the machine into the collection tray at the side, picking them up and shuffling them into a neat stack, as the machine takes more blank pages and copies.

Cameron hadn't realised how quickly paper accumulates in these files – all the CDM material, police reports and coroner's reports. Cameron quickly scans down the last document, the coroner's report, and reads *File Closed* and the date.

Suddenly, from outside the copy room, a door swings open violently, hitting the opposing wall with a thud. This is unusual for this building. Cameron opens the copy room door and looks outside. A team of FBI jacketed agents are unceremoniously searching Mitchell's office. It looks like a raid.

Jesus, they were quick, Cameron thinks to himself.

Ducking back inside the copy room, Cameron takes the last few copied files from the out tray and puts them into his case. Taking the originals from the machine, he double checks under the photocopier cover one last time.

"Fuck it," Cameron shouts in frustration. He moves to the door. He must get these files back, otherwise they'll know copies were made. The agents are still in the office and a small crowd has appeared directly outside Mitchell's office, watching and commenting on what is going on.

Cameron walks, calmly, out of the copy room and moves away from Mitchell's office. At the end of the corridor are the drink and snack machines and Cameron decides to wait here, within sight of Mitchell's office to see what is happening. It was not uncommon to see Hal Cameron hanging around the snack machine, so he felt inconspicuous.

An FBI agent emerges carrying a large A4 folder. It is one Hal had copied earlier in the day.

"Christ," Cameron says to himself. He knows that he has to do something.

Cameron fumbles in his pocket for some change. He slots two coins into the drinks machine and presses two buttons. The agent is getting near and is walking with a determined gait, towards the elevators. Just as the agent nears, Cameron removes the hot coffee from the machine and quickly turns into the path of the oncoming agent, splashing hot coffee over both. The boiling liquid scalds the agent's hand, allowing the file to fall to the floor, scattering papers like oriental fans on the floor.

"My God! I'm so sorry!"

Cameron bends over to pick up the scattered files, while the agent wipes himself down. Unseen by the agent, Cameron mixes in the originals with what was on the floor.

"Damn it, I'm sorry. How clumsy can you be?" The great actor Lawrence Olivier would have taken notes on the performance.

"Yeah, okay, buddy. Don't worry about it."

With Cameron's help, the files are gathered on the floor and Cameron hands them back to the agent.

"Thanks."

The FBI agent continues down the corridor, glancing back only once at Cameron, pain from the scald etched in his face.

Cameron sighs with relief.

* * *

The ride down to the basement car park where Sands' car is parked is taken in silence after their brief conversation. Neither of them feels comfortable talking about it while they are still in the building. The customary bell ringing and the doors sliding open announce their arrival at the basement car park. Sands walks out first and leads the way to her car.

"Where's your car?" Mitchell asks.

Sands points to the central section of the parking lot.

"I've had it for the day. I'm going home. You want a lift?"

Mitchell intended to go into the office.

"No, thanks. I'll grab a cab out front. I'm hooked on the adrenalin rush of riding in D.C. cabs. I missed them in Greenland."

Sands laughs.

"I'll see you back at the office tomorrow and we'll close this one down."

Sands stops at her car and opens the driver's door, throwing her handbag into the passenger seat in a well-practised movement.

Mitchell suddenly realises he is standing quite close to her.

"Friends again?" he asks Sands, who smiles enigmatically.

"Jerk face." She kisses Mitchell on the cheek and jumps into her car. The wheels screech as she heads towards the up-ramp.

Mitchell watches her go and starts to walk back towards the elevator to ride one floor up to street level.

Suddenly, another car's wheels screech as the driver exits the central bay parking area and heads for the up-ramp. Mitchell hasn't previously noticed anyone else in the car park. He looks to see who it is as the blue BMW sweeps out the wrong way and crosses his path. Mitchell stops abruptly so as not to get hit. A lone female driver looks directly ahead, ignoring Mitchell's stare.

"Wait a minute?" Mitchell is taken aback. "Hey!" he shouts after the car as it pulls away up the exit ramp.

Mitchell turns and runs after the car, slowly at first, but with increasing urgency and speed.

"Hey, you! Stop!"

Mitchell sprints as fast as he can after the BMW as it begins to climb the slope towards street level. The car stops in front of the automated security barrier, a steel shutter separating the State Department office from the rest of America. The driver's hand reaches out of the side window and places a card into the machine.

"Wait! Stop!" Mitchell screams.

The barrier begins to lift, as the driver removes her card from the machine, and the car pulls away out into the street.

"Damn it!" Mitchell forces his legs to move faster. "Oh, Jesus."

Mitchell hasn't run this fast since high school track and field try-outs. Like a scene from an *Indiana Jones* movie, the steel security shutter starts to close as Mitchell races as fast as he can up the steep ramp. He lowers his head and pushes his arms out flat and dives under the barrier with inches to spare.

"I'd like to see Hal do that!"

Mitchell gets up and looks both ways on the street. There it is! The BMW is waiting at a stoplight. Mitchell approaches cautiously. The injuries he is carrying hurt him even more now. This, and the preoccupation with the driver of the car ahead, make him unaware that traffic has to brake and swerve in the slushy conditions just to avoid hitting him.

He is almost close enough now to look through the rear window, when the lights change, and the car pulls away. Mitchell reaches out and grabs hold of the rear door handle trying to open it. It is locked. The driver swings the car hard into another lane of traffic and accelerates away. Holding on tightly to the handle, Mitchell draws his gun and smashes the side window. Car horns blare and cars pull out of the way as the car begins to swerve across lanes. Reaching in through the window, Mitchell releases the lock and opens the door. The door swings open as the driver darts in and out of the city traffic trying desperately to dislodge her unwanted passenger. Mitchell is swung out into the oncoming traffic. A large delivery van pulls out of a side turning directly in front of the car as the driver swerves again to miss the van by inches.

The BMW suddenly comes to a stop. Newtonian law takes over the driving for a brief second and Mitchell is flung forward onto the wet slushy street. The third forward roll is enough to stop the inertia and he looks back directly at the driver; this time she is staring back at him.

"Rachel?"

Rachel Simmons momentarily catches Mitchell's eye before the car is put into gear and speeds off.

* * *

The heat of the air fan above the tavern door washes over Mitchell like a blast from a furnace. He is sweating, hot and cold, and in pain, all at the same time. The bar is busy and, as far as he could tell, no one notices he had entered. A green neon light in the shape of a telephone handset flashes on the wall at the far end of the bar. Mitchell hobbles through the smoke-filled crowd to get to it. Picking the receiver up, he dials. The call connects and Mitchell waits.

"Come on – come on, answer it!" Then, "Hal, is that you?"

Mitchell wasn't sure, as the person who picks the phone up is out of breath.

"Paul, thank Christ for that. The shit has hit the fan here, boy, let me tell you." Cameron is panting.

"Shut up and listen for a moment, will you!"

Who else could it have been, Mitchell reasons, wheezing down the phone line at him?

"I'm in Oscar's. The tavern bar on the corner of 21st Street between the Academy of Science and the Federal Reserve building, you know it?"

"No, but I can find it."

"Okay, get down here fast and say nothing if you are asked."

"Well, that's easy enough, I don't know anything. Sands still pissed off at you?"

"Sands?" Mitchell realises Cameron is out of the loop. It must have been a few hours since they last spoke. "No, Sands has gone home. Listen, we can't speak on the phone. Bring everything. Do you understand what I mean?"

"I have it all here with me."

"Good, now get down here fast!"

Mitchell replaces the receiver and looks to see if anyone is listening. The Washington Commanders home channel is on the large plasma screen, with interviews and highlights of their latest win over the New England Patriots. Most of the patrons are watching. Mitchell heads to the bar. He needs a drink to ease the pain in his legs, ribs, chest, and head. Let's face it, one drink wasn't going to be enough.

Suddenly, he finds his arms are pinned to his side by someone behind him. Two, what look like, regulars then frog march him towards the men's room. A loud cheer goes up, as a touchdown scoring pass is replayed on the TV.

"Hey!" Mitchell's voice is drowned out. "What the hell's going on here?"

One of the men slightly opens his jumper, revealing a revolver grip protruding out of the top of his trouser belt. Mitchell stops struggling, letting himself be led to the restroom. The odour of urinal disinfectant blocks is powerful. The room is spotlessly clean, a credit to the owners of Oscar's. Mitchell is pushed hard into the centre of the room.

"Who are you, Patriot fans or something?" Mitchell knows he is in for a rough time, so what the hell.

"Oh, we're patriots alright, Agent Mitchell." The man who showed Mitchell his firearm draws it and points it at him. The other thug moves closer to Mitchell.

"Now wait a minute, fella." Mitchell backs off, but the room isn't big enough and he soon stops. "What's the trouble here?"

Mitchell's jacket is opened, and his gun is taken. Mitchell puts his hands up. A quick check of the booths shows that the room is empty.

"All clear."

Obviously, the one holding the gun at him is the superior.

"Stay by the door. Make sure no one else comes in."

Like a well-trained hound, the other takes up position by the door.

"Just what the hell is going on here?"

A wry smile appears on the gunman's face.

"That's the point, Paul, nothing that concerns you."

"What? Who the hell are you people?"

"But you don't take the hints, do you?"

"I don't understand."

"Maybe we didn't make it clear enough for you at the cabin."

Without warning, the man hits Mitchell hard across the face with his pistol. Mitchell spins and falls to his knees in front of a line of sinks. Blood flows freely from the burst sterile strips above his eye, onto the white tiled floor.

"I suppose some people aren't receptive to new ideas, are they?"

The man punches Mitchell hard in the left kidney. Mitchell crumples to the floor.

"You must learn to read the signs, Paul. Life's a learning

experience. You either live and learn, or you don't live long."

The man looks down at Mitchell's crumpled body on the floor. Pulling back his leg, he kicks Mitchell hard in the ribs. The man guarding the door looks back into the room, as Mitchell groans in pain.

"Someone's coming. Let's go!" His accent is Russian.

"I hope this has been an educational experience for you, Paul. If you don't leave well enough alone, we may come back and test you on what you've learnt today."

The man adjusts his shirt, turns, and walks away, leaving Mitchell clutching his torso and groaning. The Russian-speaking man tosses Mitchell's gun back at him and it slides across the floor, stopping next to his head. Without looking back, the two men exit the washroom.

Mitchell slowly pulls himself up onto the sink and looks into the washbasin mirror. Blood is streaming down his face and his body is in terrible pain. He struggles to his feet and picks up his gun. Grabbing handfuls of paper towels, Mitchell tries to stem the flow of blood and tidy himself up.

* * *

Hal Cameron swiftly passes through the blanket of hot air guarding the entrance to Oscar's Tavern and is immediately sideswiped by two men as they leave in an obvious hurry. Cameron is knocked against the entrance doorway.

"Hey, watch it, dickheads!" Cameron shouts after them.

One of the men turns and glares back at Cameron who takes up the challenge by opening up his chest and shoulders to confront them.

"You want some of me, fuck face?"

The man starts back towards Cameron but is held back by the other.

"Leave him, we have to go."

"Russian?" Cameron notes the accent with surprise.

"Who won the fucking Cold War anyway?" he shouts out, mainly to himself, as the men have already gone. Cameron moves further into the bar.

Mitchell splashes water onto his face. The cold water stings, but he has managed to stop the bleeding. He raises his head and looks at his reflection in the mirror. His face has acquired a new cut, and the bruising is worse now. His left eye needed no encouragement to close after his jeep was hit by a snow plough and now a pistol whipping has pushed it over the edge. It is shut and swollen.

The door to the men's room swings open and two loud, boisterous men enter. Mitchell stands upright, the best he can, trying to give an air of normality about his actions. He turns off the running water, giving a momentary glance at the young men, as they pass him by. Mitchell wipes and dries his face with more paper towels. Turning, he leaves the washroom a bit dirtier than when he arrived.

Mitchell walks unsteadily towards the bar. Reaching out to take a seat, a hand grabs his shoulder. Out of instinct, Mitchell turns, fist drawn back in readiness to strike – Hal Cameron's smiling face turns to one of shock.

"Jesus H. Christ, Paul. What the fuck happened to you?"

Mitchell lowers his arm and Cameron sees his injured face more clearly.

"I've been trying to fight my way to the bar all evening." Mitchell smiles, but the smile is cut short by having to cough.

"Christ, Paul. I'll take you to a hospital. You should get checked out." Cameron takes Mitchell by the arm, trying to lead him away.

"I'm alright, Hal, you should see the other guy. I bet his

fists are really buzzing now. Just get me a drink, will yah?"

"Don't be a fucking hero, you need medical attention."

"I just need a few minutes, okay?"

Cameron looks at him with concern. "Alright then, you get a seat and I'll get us some alcoholic medicine."

Mitchell nods in thanks, turning to look for a seat. Cameron watches him disappear into the crowd before he starts to push his way towards the bar. Mitchell moves gingerly through the mêlée of sports fans cheering every tackle and hit the Washington defence inflict on New England's offensive line.

Mitchell tries to protect his hurting body from any stray elbows and arms. Finding an unoccupied booth, he stumbles onto the seat with a groan of pain and a slow release of air as his muscles can finally give in for a bit of relief.

Cameron soon appears at the table, carrying a bottle of whiskey and two glasses, and seats himself opposite Mitchell.

Cameron motions to the bottle on the table. "Anaesthetic."

"God bless you." Mitchell reaches for the glass Cameron has just poured for him. He swallows it down in one go. "Ahh, that's the medicine I like to take."

Cameron pours two more glasses of whiskey. Mitchell takes his but, before he drinks, he holds the glass up in the air.

"May your camels have triplets. Cheers."

Both men empty their glasses.

"So, what the hell kind of rumble were you in this time?" Cameron enquires.

"An uneven one – two hairy-ass apes frog marched me into the washroom and said I should back off."

"Let me guess, two well-dressed phone booths in black suits, one with a Russian accent. Am I right?"

"Yeah – how did you know?"

"I met them on the way in – now, having seen you, my New Year's resolution is to only box people below my own weight."

"What?" Mitchell is unaware of Cameron's bravado earlier.

"What the hell's going on, Paul? The Feds have ransacked your office and Sands has pulled the rug on the entire investigation, what's going on?"

"Something, I'm not sure what yet, but it's massive. One thing is for certain, I'm getting close and hold on to your draws, Mrs. Robinson…" Mitchell suffers a twinge of pain in his ribs as he breathes in and downs another swig of whiskey from his glass.

"What?" Cameron urges Mitchell on.

"Rachel Simmons is not dead."

"Say what?" Cameron's mouth is now wide open.

"I said, Simmons is not dead. In fact, she's very much alive, driving around town in a light blue BMW."

"I don't understand." Cameron is shaking his head, perplexed.

"She even tried to run me down, outside this tavern tonight."

"Alive? But you saw her shot. I mean, shot people normally stay dead, right?" Cameron is thinking aloud.

"She must have called someone after I spotted her. Those two bozos knew of the shooting in St. Lawrence. Gave me the impression they were the ones doing the shooting."

"Okay, let's say she's alive and you saw her tonight. Why the shooting? Why play dead?"

"I don't know. Those bullets felt real enough to me." Mitchell shook his head slightly to help his reasoning process. "I was set up by people who know how to do these things."

"What, like the CIA? You are saying the CIA is involved in this thing too?"

Mitchell shrugs his shoulders as he pours himself another glass.

"We should call Sands," Cameron continues.

"No!" Mitchell lowers his voice, as a few customers in the bar look over towards the booth. "No, Hal. Sands wants me off this as well, for different reasons, I hope."

"Okay then, where does that leave us?"

"If Simmons' death was faked, it was to throw me off the trail. Spotting her must have thrown a wrench in the machinery." Mitchell pauses as his mind takes a deep dive into his thoughts. "Simmons, or whoever she is, was at the cabin just in case Hunter came back. She was there to take care of him. Tidy up a loose end."

"Simmons must be the one pulling all the strings," Cameron offers a solution.

Mitchell thinks for a moment. "Possibly. Listen, I bet that when the NSA got involved in Kensington's death, it was something they, whoever they are, didn't count on – me doing a very thorough investigation."

"You mean, Sands was never meant to assign you?"

"Sands should never have been in the loop, someone screwed up." Mitchell was getting excited as he felt sure the coin was about to drop. "I was never supposed to find that imprint of the suicide note in Kensington's house. They missed it, I didn't. They've been trying to cover their asses ever since."

"What about Simmons?"

"Was it Simmons or a doppelganger? If a phony Simmons, then it was a fake assassination, choreographed, squib hits the lot, and now this little talk Sands and I have just had at State – it is all crap. I don't give a damn what they say, this is all just to keep me from finding something out."

"But what?" Cameron asks.

"It has to do with the Cold Dark Matter project, that's the common denominator. It was just their bad luck I saw Simmons in her car tonight."

"Her bad luck or yours?" Cameron points to Mitchell's battered face.

"I see your point." Mitchell nurses his eye.

"So, they fake her death to throw you off the trail of Hunter, is that it?"

"She may be the real Rachel Simmons; did you ever think about that? An agent planted in the CDM team."

Cameron looks bewildered.

"Think about it, I was suckered into going up to find Hunter. They knew he wasn't there, but the investigation led me there." Mitchell takes his drink and blood mixes with the liquid from his mouth, as he sips from the glass. "There must have been a dozen people in the loop who could have stopped me before I got on that flight. But they didn't. They kept Simmons there just so they could fake that hit, making me be believe that she was killed. Could your average scientist pull that off, without at least some black ops training?"

"Simmons, or whoever she is, is working for – who then?"

"The same people who took the suicide note from Kensington's study, the imprint I shouldn't have found."

Cameron mulls over what he has just heard. "Medvedenko, surely not him and his family too? That all happened in Russia, for Christ's sake!"

Mitchell shrugs his shoulders, which hurt too. Both men sit in silence, bewildered at their blue sky thinking of the Cold Dark Matter problem. Cameron breaks the silence.

"It's all plausible, I guess. Listen, I'm not sure about any of this, but you must be getting close otherwise they wouldn't have gone to all this trouble. Whatever it is, they want it kept secret. They're willing to kill for it. Maybe even you and if that isn't the real Simmons you saw tonight, the real Rachel Simmons is still out there, somewhere, and in danger."

"Good Christ, don't you think I know that!"

Mitchell is exhausted, in pain and the whiskey is making him aggressive and sleepy at the same time. Cameron shakes his head.

"Man, we're way out of our depth here."

"Not yet we're not. In the morning, I'm going to pay Professor Lawrence another visit. I've got one or two questions I'd like to ask him."

"You think you are up to it?" Cameron is concerned.

"I will be once you drop me at the emergency room."

Mitchell takes another long swig from his glass, as Cameron looks bewildered into his.

Chapter Six

Miss Bunker, the acerbic receptionist Professor Lawrence used as his first line of defence at the Science Grant Allocation Unit, is not at her desk.

Good, Mitchell thinks. He has had enough fights to last him a lifetime. The door to Lawrence's office is closed, but Mitchell is in no mood to dance the Potomac Two-Step; the right channels, appointments cancelled. Mitchell pauses briefly outside the door, then, without knocking, he enters.

Astonishment and bewilderment both smack Mitchell in the face as he steps into an empty office. Immediately he doubles back and checks he is on the right floor and office.

I am, this is where I was.

"If I'm not careful, I could end up paranoid and talking to myself here," he mumbles.

Mitchell goes to the main reception to get answers on where Lawrence is now. The lobby of the Treasury Offices is how he remembered it. The general enquiry desk was in the middle of the grand rotunda and the treasury emblem of scales over a blue chevron and key are marked out in mosaic tiling on the marble floor. The receptionist at enquires is busy with what looks like a businessman. Mitchell arrives to hear the end of the conversation.

"I'm sorry sir."

Are all government receptionists trained to speak in such a condescending manner? Mitchell wonders.

"No, you can't pay your taxes here. You fill out the forms and send a banker's draft or do it all online."

Mitchell looks at the businessman and, on closer inspection, he is not all he seems to be. His raincoat covers up an old suit and shirt, and his shoes are muddy.

"That's a real pity, young lady." The Southern accent is heavy, but Mitchell can't say whether it is east or west of the Mississippi.

"I have my taxes in the truck outside, six sacks of nickels looking for a home, save you taking mine."

"I'm sorry sir, like I said—"

"I know, I know. Fill out the forms and send a banker's draft. Trouble is, Miss, I can't write nor read and there ain't no bank in my town."

"Sorry, sir, just fill out the forms," the receptionist repeats.

The man gives up and walks away.

"Yes?" The receptionist rings the bell for round two and the next fight to begin.

"Professor Lawrence of the Science Grant Allocation Unit – where might I find him?"

"Professor Lawrence? One moment, I'll just check for you."

The receptionist types expertly on her computer keyboard. Mitchell can hear a loud bleep every time the receptionist presses the return key.

"I'm sorry, sir, we have no record of any Professor Lawrence having an office in this building. Are you sure you are in the right department?"

"That's impossible, I was here a few days ago, I met him right here, in this building."

Mitchell is reassuring himself, more than convincing the receptionist.

"Please, check again."

The receptionist once again types onto her computer keypad, but the dead-end bleep of a computer not able to process any further information resonates within the confined enquiry desk workstation.

"I'm sorry, sir. According to our records, there has never been a Professor Lawrence in residence here. In fact," the receptionist taps additional keys on her computer, "there are no records of a Professor Lawrence ever being attached to a science grant allocations unit."

Mitchell thanks the receptionist as he turns to walk away. How could this be? People and whole departments just can't vanish.

Unnoticed by Mitchell, a man dressed in a long, black overcoat is watching him leave. The man takes a cigar from his inside coat pocket and finds a match in another, lifting his right leg he strikes the match off his black, highly stylised patent leather shoe. The man steps outside of the building once his cigar has been lighted.

* * *

Mitchell climbs the last few steps to the third floor of Alvin Hawks' apartment building as if they were the last few steps to the summit of Mount Everest. The adage of 'it's not the years but the mileage' sprung to mind and how true it was.

The notice at the top of the landing indicates the room numbers and which direction visitors would need to go to find them. Hawks is in apartment #309, to the right.

Apartment #309 is the last door on the floor, at the end of the corridor. That meant, in this Washington Project 2000-built apartment, the fire escape and alarmed window that accessed it are situated at the end of the corridor too. *I bet Hawks chose this apartment himself*, Mitchell reasons.

Hawks always had an escape route plan while he was a hacker. If the security system of a programme he was hacking into started to run a trace on him, Hawks would have a quick escape programme standing by to sever any traceable links within nanoseconds. This apartment fits Hawks' profile like a glove.

Music is coming from behind Hawks' door. Someone is home. Listening for a moment, Mitchell suddenly realises he recognises the music. The rhythmic booming of Rick Savage's bass from Def Leppard is unmistakable. British heavy metal bands are big the world over, but no more so than in Greenland. Mitchell could even place the album: *Pyromania*. He astounds even himself with his trivia knowledge.

Mitchell knocks and waits. There is no reply, so he knocks louder, this time with his fist. The music goes off.

"Who is it?" Hawks tries to sound bigger than he is.

"Alvin, it's Paul Mitchell. Open up, I need to talk with you."

The door remains resolutely shut.

"What do you want?" Hawks' voice takes its more natural form, which is at least a pitch higher in tone.

"Alvin, open up. It's me, Paul."

"Listen, I, er, I have company, you know, a lady, and, well, you understand, don't you, man?"

Mitchell is totally unconvinced, knowing Hawks better than anyone else in the agency. Hawks must be up to something dodgy otherwise he wouldn't be this jittery.

The window fire escape is why Hawks has obviously picked this apartment: an escape route. Mitchell goes to the window and looks at the seals. There is a warning sign letting visitors know that the window is alarmed, which is a deterrent to stop the windows being opened in hot weather, allowing non-desirables to enter unnoticed. However, the alarm outside

Hawks' room has been subtlety deactivated. But you would need to know what to look for to spot it.

Mitchell opens the window to silence. No alarm bells are ringing. He smiles. Climbing out onto the iron grill platform, he looks up. Two boots appear just above his head, and they descend the metal ladder which Hawks has climbed onto from a side window in his apartment. Mitchell waits silently, unnoticed by Hawks, until they are standing together on the platform.

"You know, Alvin…"

Hawks jumps in surprise.

"You should take more care of yourself. Didn't your mother tell you, you could catch pneumonia coming out in weather like this, especially after a shower? You'd best go back into the warm."

"You know, I think you're absolutely right, Mr. Mitchell, sir."

Mitchell smiles and follows Hawks back up the way he came.

Hawks was eighteen when Mitchell first encountered him. The New York State Educational Exam Board computer system was being hacked into. Final grades were being randomly altered, always higher. It took a while to track Hawks down back then, as he never altered his own grades. He never needed to, as he was already an A student and therefore the shadow of suspicion never fell across his name. That didn't happen until Governor McKenzie's son, Brandon, widely understood not to be the sharpest tack in the box, started to get As in every subject he took. After much soul searching by his father and the allegations that he was buying his son an education, Mitchell extracted a confession from Brandon and he fingered Hawks, who was selling pass grades to all those who could afford to pay him. Mitchell liked the irony – the nerd, always put down and set upon, fleecing the rich jocks to give them grades he himself could achieve in his sleep.

That was ten years ago. Now Hawks was nearing his thirties, but he still looked like the geek college kid Mitchell busted way back then. He was a perpetual teenager, but without question the best computer analyst working outside of the NSA.

Hawks flops down in an armchair with the expression of a chastised teen written on his face. In his baggy open denim shirt, baggy black Iron Maiden T-shirt and loose-fitting jeans that clung mysteriously well to the Lagrange point between the top of his hips and top of his thighs, Hawks is dressed like every parent's teenage nightmare. His thin wispy goatee is, if needed, the icing on the cake.

Hawks' apartment is as expected. The carpet had made valiant efforts, in random places, to emerge from beneath a thick layer of books, computer magazines and takeaway food containers.

However, in the corner of the room, still switched on with a flashing warning notice, sits a computer set up worthy of any university information technology lab. The notice on the computer flashes 'System Files Deleted'.

"Covering your tracks, Alvin?"

"Just getting rid of old data, Mr. Mitchell," Hawks assures him.

"That's okay with me." Mitchell sits on a breakfast barstool near what was once a breakfast bar, but which is now home to two pairs of rather old basketball shoes. "Listen, Alvin, I need your help."

Hawks shows no sign of interest.

"Interested?" Mitchell continues.

Hawks replies, without looking at Mitchell, "What kind of help?"

"Technical."

"Computer systems?"

"I might ask you to look in a few, yes."

"Are you mad? That's how we met in the first place. Besides, I don't do that anymore, security is too tight on secure sites."

"Don't give me that bullshit, you told me yourself that no system is ever fully secure."

"Maybe I was wrong."

Mitchell leans back a little on the stool, with a knowing look on his face.

"How much money did I earn last year, Alvin?"

"How should I know?"

"You do know, don't you? And you know where my house is, what bank I use, even where I went on holiday last June."

"You didn't go in June; you went in July." Hawks smiles to himself; the smile disappears quickly with the realisation of his mistake. "Fuck it!"

"You never could resist showing off, could you?"

"But secure systems are far more sophisticated these days, especially if you're talking about NSA secure network. You have point of interface tracking, offensive anti-virus viruses that use the input signal to attack the depositing computer system, all kinds of shit like that."

"We upgraded our systems because of you, Alvin."

"I did my time for that."

"You did five months' community service, Alvin."

"Al."

"What?"

"No one calls me Alvin anymore, except, perhaps, my grandmother. Please, it's Al."

"Okay, Al."

"Why should I help you? You're the one who got me into trouble in the first place."

"You got yourself into trouble. I just caught you."

"That just gives me all the more reason."

Mitchell thought. "If you help me with this, I'll see what I can do about bringing you in from the cold to work for me full time. You know what that would mean, don't you?"

Hawks is thinking.

"That's right, Al, your record wiped clean, your own computer lab with a budget you could only dream of, a salary, government pension and health package, the works. You're not getting any younger, Al, think of the future."

Mitchell knows, above all else, the prospect of working in an NSA computer lab, with all the resources the NSA has at its disposal, is a hacker's wet dream.

"You mean it?"

"Sure, the full Monty."

"But what if you're, I don't know, killed or fired or something. What about me then?"

"I'll tell Hal Cameron about our deal, and he'll keep my promise. Fair enough?"

"Okay, I'll do it." Mitchell smiles. "When do I get my badge and gun?" Hawks asks enthusiastically.

Mitchell looks to the heavens, rolls his eyes, and shakes his head. Perhaps there was someone else he should have asked after all.

* * *

Mitchell and Hawks wait patiently by the automated security barrier in the State Department building's underground car park. It was a simple matter of presenting his NSA ID to gain access to the building and Hawks, using a pseudonym, signed in as a visitor.

It seemed an age, especially in the cold biting wind that swirled through the concrete labyrinth below Constitution

Avenue, before a car approached the barrier to exit. Watching, out of sight from the driver in an unlit alcove, Mitchell and Hawks observe the routine of inserting a security pass into the automated barrier machine to open the steel gate. Earlier, Hawks had secured, by magnets at the rear of the machine, a small digital transmitter. Its only sign of activity is a small green light by the power switch. The barrier door opens and Hawks looks down to the small portable laptop computer resting on his lap. The dim glow of the LCD screen gives Hawks' face a bluish radiance.

"Well?" Mitchell whispers impatiently.

The blue light across Hawks' face is now broken with streaks of black as information starts to download into his laptop from the security barrier.

"It's working," Hawks excitedly reports back. "Name, address, title, security level, everything."

Mitchell pats Hawks on the shoulder. "Well done, Al."

"Magnetic strips, you've got to love them." Hawks beams to Mitchell.

Another car pulls up, to enter the car park this time. Soon the information about the driver starts to come onto Hawks' computer screen.

"How did you come up with this little idea?" Mitchell watches as Hawks creates an automated computer log.

"Easy really. The only electronic information people carry around with them is stored on magnetic strips, credit cards, banker's cards, and office IDs, etcetera. It's convenient, but also archaic – it's the twenty-first century, for Christ's sake. Magnetic strips are 1970s technology. It makes it easy to read."

"Everything with a magnetic strip is read by this gadget?"

"Oh, sure. I figured you would know that being NSA."

Jesus, Mitchell thought. *What chance has Joe Public got?*

The sound of rubber stops their conversation as another car pulls up to the barrier to exit.

"This is her," Mitchell whispers to Hawks, who briefly looks up from his screen to see what Mitchell is so animated about.

The damaged BMW pulls up to the barrier. Inside, Mitchell can see Simmons placing her card into the barrier's console. Mitchell looks down at Hawks as the black streaks of information pass across his face.

"Lockhart, Julia. She's CIA." Hawks looks up to Mitchell.

"CIA?"

* * *

Wheaton is a small suburb about an hour's drive north of the capital. Most of the top companies based in Washington have houses here for their senior managers and their families. The schools and parks are all excellent and the crime rate is nothing like that of the city.

Julia Lockhart stops her car on the road outside a modest, double-fronted detached house in the newest part of town and gets out. The white shiplap boarding that defines the houses in this area has collected a recent snowfall and Lockhart can't help but smile with pride at her own little chocolate box dream home. Lockhart reaches into her handbag for the door key. It is dark and she waves a hand at the porch light sensor.

"Hello," she calls out to the sensor and the light comes on as she nears.

She finds the key below a pocketbook and, taking it, opens the door. Just as she does, a hand quickly clamps over her mouth, and she is pushed quickly inside.

Mitchell forces her into the hall, keeping his hand over her mouth. Al Hawks closes the door behind them, making sure they are not seen. Mitchell speaks softly.

"Are you alone?"

Lockhart nods yes.

"You cause me trouble and it will be your last act on Earth. You understand?"

Mitchell slowly takes his hand away from her mouth and reaches around inside her overcoat, withdrawing her service revolver from her hip. Stepping away from her, he quickly moves to the living room windows and looks out at the street. Satisfied that no one saw them, he draws the curtains. Mitchell turns and flicks on the light switch. For a long while, Mitchell and Lockhart stare at each other like scorned lovers.

"I'm thirsty," Hawks breaks the silence. "Anyone want a coke?" Hawks doesn't wait for a reply and heads off to find the kitchen.

"You had best start explaining, lady, I want some straight answers to some straight questions. No bullshit because I know enough now to know when I'm being lied to."

Lockhart moves into the living room and sits on the arm of a sofa near the door.

"Why were you impersonating Rachel Simmons?" Mitchell asks first.

Lockhart shakes her head. "If you knew as much as you claim, you wouldn't need me to tell you."

"Don't push your luck, Lockhart, you're already on thin ice with me."

"Don't threaten me!" Lockhart laughs softly. "You have no fucking idea, do you? You were set up from the beginning. That's right, from day one. This was a CIA operation from the outset. Come on, Paul, an NSA agent based in Greenland assigned to investigate a suicide in Maryland, come on, wake up and smell the coffee!"

Mitchell sits down on a chair by the window and at the same time his shoulders sink a little lower. Lockhart continues.

"You were far better in the field than they gave you credit

for; they wanted you out of the picture and any ideas you may have had they would have rubbished."

"Since when did the CIA start pulling the strings of the NSA?"

Hawks appears at the doorway. "You're joking, right?" Hawks adds.

"The public face of the CIA – never." Lockhart emphasises the statement with a sweep of her hand. "It couldn't possibly. The oversight committee chairmen would run to *The Washington Post* screaming their heads off, looking forward to the time when they retire and join the lecture circuit – 'How I brought down the secret cabal inside the CIA.'." Lockhart pauses momentarily, fixing Mitchell straight in the eye. "However, CIA black operations are a different matter."

"Does black ops include roughing up NSA agents?"

"What?"

"Your two pals at Oscar's Tavern, they tried very hard to kick several types of shit out of me."

"I don't know anything about that."

Mitchell studies Lockhart's face. She looks sincere, but she also looked dead a few days ago.

"If you can't tell me the truth, then don't insult my intelligence by lying to me."

"I mean it, I know nothing about it."

"So, the CIA, in its infinite wisdom, doesn't consult you on every move it makes, but I assure you, I didn't do this shaving." Mitchell points to his bruised and battered face.

"Paul, if it were black ops, you wouldn't be here now. Just doesn't sound like their style."

"They haven't got a style. They just do whatever they are told to do to get the job done, right?"

"All the same…"

"I can't force you to tell me anything, as I don't have the

CIA travel agency number to book you on a rendition flight." Mitchell stands up and adjusts his overcoat. "You can tell your superiors that this is not over by a long way."

Mitchell walks to the hall where Hawks is standing.

"You know I might have backed off if the red tape and the bullshit got high enough, but now, no way – fuck the lot of you."

Mitchell motions to Hawks that they are leaving. As the front door opens and Mitchell starts to step out, the external security light switches on. Mitchell looks out to the street and abruptly stops. A black Ford car pulls up directly behind Lockhart's car on her driveway. Mitchell takes a step back into the doorway of the house and the porch light switches off. Hawks runs into the back of Mitchell.

"What's up, doc?" Hawks asks.

Mitchell doesn't reply but instead he backs into the house, forcing Hawks back inside too. Mitchell closes the door, leaving just enough of a gap to watch the car out front. Two figures emerge from the car and walk calmly to the rear of their car.

"What is it?" Lockhart joins them at the door.

"I have no idea," Hawks whispers in reply, "something out there has spooked him."

"Paul?" Lockhart tries to move Mitchell aside to look outside.

"This doesn't feel right, get back inside the house."

Mitchell pushes her back. The two figures begin to walk towards the house. Mitchell strains his eyes to see them through the darkness; each seem to be carrying two long objects that are silhouetted by the street lighting. Mitchell closes the door and puts the security chain on.

"Whoever they are, they are coming right here. Are you expecting anyone?" Mitchell whispers to Lockhart.

"No." She is now anxious too.

The halogen bulbs of the security light flash on and Mitchell quickly looks through the security camera in the door to see who these people are. Standing on the lawn, momentarily dazzled by the light, are the two thugs who had beaten him up in the tavern bar earlier; both are carrying shotguns.

"Oh shit!"

"What is it?" both Lockhart and Hawks ask simultaneously.

"Do you know these two?" Mitchell moves aside to allow Lockhart the chance to look through the door camera.

"No, never seen them before. Who are they?"

"The two thugs who beat me up earlier."

Mitchell looks back through the camera and sees both men calmly raise their shotguns and aim it at the house.

"Jesus Christ, get down!"

Mitchell dives to the floor as Hawks and Lockhart scramble to the living room.

The blast from one shotgun makes a hole the size of a soccer ball in the door, showering Mitchell with splinters of wood as he crawls away. Other rounds now begin to systematically rip into the windows, walls, and front door of the house. Mitchell crawls on his stomach into the living room and shelters behind the now up-turned sofa.

"Who the fuck are these guys?" Hawks shouts over the explosion of shells and items of furniture they are hitting.

Mitchell draws his .45 colt automatic, pulling the breech back and cocking the pistol.

"Here we go again."

He looks towards Lockhart, who is crawling towards him on her stomach.

"What the fuck is going on?" she screams.

Wood and glass explode around their heads as more shotgun shells rip through the room.

"Don't you know? It seems every time I pay you a visit, someone tries to kill me."

One of the gunmen runs past the side window and Mitchell fires four rounds at the running figure.

"Not jealous lovers of yours, are they?"

Hawks stumbles over Lockhart to get away from a hotspot of incoming firepower.

Suddenly, there is a lull in the firing. Lockhart sees her own gun lying on the floor next to the upturned sofa and picks it up. She quickly moves to the window and peeks outside.

"They're reloading," she says while checking her own Smith & Wesson .38 for rounds.

"I don't know who the hell they are," she exclaims again.

The brief lull in the fire fight ends abruptly with a deluge of shells raining into the living room.

"Who the fuck are they?" Hawks asks again, as glass from the living room windows shatters and flies over them both.

"You want me to go out there and fucking ask them?" Mitchell snaps back at Hawks. "Come on, I've had about enough of this shit."

Mitchell starts to crawl along the floor towards the hallway, followed by Hawks and Lockhart. Wood, plaster, and glass continue to fall around them as their attackers start to move in closer, firing as they come.

"Come on, up here."

Mitchell crawls to the stairs and climbs over the debris of glass and plaster to the relative safety of the upstairs. Once again, the house falls silent from gunfire.

"Reloading," Hawks calls out.

In the distance, Mitchell can hear sirens. Lockhart spots a flashlight downstairs.

"Look!" she whispers loudly. Mitchell and Hawks peer through the banisters to look down the stairs. The beam pierces the darkness of the living room, randomly searching and prying the darkness with the beam of light.

Mitchell and Lockhart look at each other. The sound of her front door crashing open makes them both jump; Lockhart's eyes are wide with fear.

"Is there another way out of here?"

"No." Lockhart shakes her head.

"Oh, great," Hawks says in a voice just barely concealing the panic he feels.

"He brought us up here!" Lockhart points to Mitchell.

"How many rounds have you got?" Mitchell asks.

Lockhart flips open the cylinder of her .38 Revolver. "Five."

"I've got a full clip. Not enough, damn," Mitchell offers.

"What? What do you mean not enough?" Hawks' face is puzzled. "We can't afford to get into a fire fight with them."

Mitchell slides the full clip into the grip of his pistol. "It's never like this in the movies," he mumbles to himself.

Like an iron door slamming shut, the little ambient light that was filtering through the house from the two or three nearby streetlights goes off. The house is plunged into total blackness.

"They've got the lights," Hawks whispers.

Mitchell feels for the banister rail which he knows is somewhere just in front of him. Finding the familiar smooth glossy finish of the woodwork, he places his head against the upright columns and looks down. After a few seconds, his eyes, pupils wide open, spot two soft green lights positioned the same distance apart as you would expect from night vision goggles.

"Night vision goggles," Mitchell reports back to the others.

There is a creak on the stairs below them.

It is debatable which of the five senses is the most valuable. To have them all functioning beautifully is the ideal state to be in, of course. But most of the world's population has a deficiency with one or more, this being underlined, as his college professor kept reminding him in his economics class, by diet and social economic background. Eyesight, hearing, smell, taste, or sound? It all depends on the circumstances in which you need to rely on them, Mitchell had surmised. His brief spell at Fort Bragg's Special Operations Counter-Terrorism Unit had also taught him to use alternate senses when one or more were 'erased'. Being blindfolded and tied to a chair for hours helped Mitchell strengthen his other senses of hearing and smell so he could note who was in the room with him, male or female, and where they were standing or moving. Mitchell also marvelled that his mind could recall all this information with a single spark of a neurotransmitter impulse in his brain. The human body is a miracle of evolution, or creation, depending on your education.

Lockhart touches his leg, and her hand moves up his body to his chest. Mitchell knows it is Lockhart by her perfume and he puts his hand over her mouth to silence her.

The noise from Al Hawks' head thumping into Mitchell's would have woken the dead – well, it sounds like it and sure as hell feels like it! The pain is intense round Mitchell's cut and swollen eye, and he starts to feel a warm trickle touch his cheek. Despite the pain both he and Hawks were in, the adrenalin quells any urge to cry out.

Mitchell crawls forward with Lockhart and Hawks in tow, clinging sloth-like to his frame.

* * *

Image enhancement technology has progressed quickly within the last decade, but Mitchell knows the science well. Using amplified infrared and visible light, this piece of kit is now a standard issue to US frontline troops worldwide. He needs to get to a place where infrared and visible light would be at its weakest, and he needs to get there fast.

The strange and alien world that inhabits night vision is predominately green in colour; black and white add little to the palate but help define the material world outside of the all- encompassing mask of the wearer. The colours red and blue betray the physical world in this domain and these two agent provocateurs of the spectrum are the most sought after.

The door flings open on its hinges and the green world inside reveals a bedroom. The cold black outline of a savage pump-action shotgun scans the room for red or blue. Nothing. The sound of splintered wood makes the green world spin sharply 180º, and suddenly the distinctive glow of red and blue fills the screen. It was expected.

Closer now, the material shapes inside the room define it. A rectangular cubicle in the far corner, a low metal tub to the left, and a low seat, all cold in nature indicated this was a bathroom. But there was something else in here, a noise – water, running water, and it was coming from the cubicle.

Mitchell is getting wet and a little warm, although his clothing is giving him some protection from the hot water. He knows the water is now visible in the infrared and it isn't long until the green cat's eyes reflect the interest in the shower he was taking. The red waves of heat flow up into the air like a desert mirage. The cubicle wobbles in a slow motion dance of thermal images, which are undefined, random, and obscure. Just what Mitchell is hoping for.

A pair of green cat's eyes nears the cubicle door and, taking a deep breath and building his entire body into one tight muscle, Mitchell throws the door open, smashing it as hard as he can into the intruder. The impact shatters the glass door, and the intruder falls heavily to the ground. Diving out of the shower, Mitchell lands forcefully on top of him and gropes for his mask, yanking and twisting as hard as he can. The crack of ripped vertebra and the involuntary leg spasm signal the intruder's crossing into unconsciousness.

The shotgun blast rips the ceramic tiles from the walls in an explosion of splinters, spraying out across the room like a lethal fan. The house lights suddenly come on and the green world is struck as if a solar flare smashes into it, blinding white light burns the retinas of his eyes. Mitchell and Lockhart's service revolvers take aim, firing four rapid shots from each gun into his torso. Like wheat caught in a summer breeze, the gunman's body twists and rises under the hail of bullets before slumping dead to the ground.

"Come on!" Hawks calls from the doorway. "The police are here!"

Lockhart emerges from a walk-in cupboard. The holes in the louvred door neatly exhibit the bunching of her shots. Mitchell looks down at the face of the man underneath him. It is the Russian-speaking man from the washroom at Oscar's bar. He gets up and wipes the blood from his weeping eye, then, grabbing a towel from a nearby hot rail, he tries to stop the bleeding.

Looking down at the towel, he shakes his head.

"This is never going to heal."

Mitchell looks up at Hawks rubbing a bruise on his forehead.

"Sorry, boss," is all he can muster as the police sirens outside draw to a halt.

* * *

The street directly outside Julia Lockhart's house is alive with cars. Police officers are squatting behind their open car doors, pointing various armaments at Mitchell, Lockhart, and Hawks. Suddenly, a million-candlelight beam lights the house up like a Super Trouper light at a Broadway show.

"Drop your guns and put your hands up where we can see them."

The familiar, yet anxious, call of the duty sergeant needs no further explanation. Mitchell and Lockhart drop their guns, with pleasure, and raise their hands. Hawks already has his hands on his head.

"Okay, now walk slowly towards this car." The sergeant's voice, even through the megaphone, sounds relieved that his suspects are doing as they are told.

Walking side by side with Hawks following nervously behind, Mitchell and Lockhart arrive at the police car.

"I'm NSA and she's CIA; we both have identification," Mitchell informs the sergeant as three junior officers come from behind cars and cover them with their pistols.

"Is that right, now?" the police sergeant replies.

Is every police sergeant in America of Irish decent? Mitchell wonders.

"And I'm Clark Kent."

And a comedian? Mitchell hopes that was said with his inner monologue.

Without warning, the side glass panel of the police car shatters. Mitchell and Lockhart duck and turn to look back at the house. The Russian is walking from the house, blood streaming down his nose, his neck held in a contorted position by his shoulders, gun raised and firing.

The three officers standing closest are downed by single shots as Mitchell grabs Lockhart, throws her over the hood of the police car and follows her for cover, picking up a handgun from one of the officers. Hawks crawls to the back of the car.

"Jesus, Jesus."

Confusion reigns as the Russian opens fire, this time with a semi-automatic machine gun.

"Get in!"

Mitchell grabs Lockhart by the scruff of the neck and throws her into the passenger seat of the sergeant's police car. The Russian runs for cover to his own car, as the police return fire. Inside, with the door closed, Mitchell watches in disbelief as if without a care in the world the Russian calmly takes his neck in both hands and twists it violently back into position. Police round after round harmlessly ricochet off his car, like bugs off a windscreen.

"Bullet proof?"

Mitchell slams the car into gear and pulls away.

"Hey, wait for me!"

Looking in the side mirror, Mitchell sees Hawks waving his hands and he stops. As soon as Hawks jumps in, the car pulls away fast.

"Who'd a thought I would ever hail a police car?" Hawks looks out of the rear window. "He's coming!"

"What?" Lockhart looks back out of the rear window too. The Russian has started his car and is pursuing them.

"I thought you took him out back in the house?"

"No one seems to stay dead for long these days," Mitchell says, with more than a touch of irony in his voice.

* * *

Snow falls on the windscreen and the sticky flakes reduce the visibility further as the wipers smear the snow. The washers are frozen and useless.

"He's gaining on us, Paul," says Hawks, still looking out of the back of the car window, "step on it!"

"Drive to my office; we'll be safe there," Lockhart insists.

"The lion's den, oh, sure we will. This goon back there is probably on his way over there now to get reinforcements," Hawks shouts.

"I agree, we can't be sure of anyone anymore," Mitchell adds.

"What about me?" Lockhart asks.

"They want you out of the equation just as much as me now."

Mitchell switches on the police radio.

"*The two vehicles are now heading west on University Boulevard towards Forrest Glenn. I repeat, police vehicle 435 has been carjacked and is now being driven by suspects wanted in relation to a police shooting. A black Ford vehicle with D.C. plates seen heading in the same direction is also wanted for questioning – repeat, we have officers down at the scene. All occupants are armed and dangerous, proceed with extreme caution… Dispatch out.*"

"Shit!" Hawks exclaims. "The cops are after us now too!"

Mitchell stares ahead at the road, deep in thought. Suddenly, the car lurches forward, making both Mitchell and Lockhart jerk forward.

"What the hell?"

Without warning, the car is jolted forwards again. This time the car slides on the icy road surface and Mitchell has to fight to keep the car straight.

"Where is he, Al?" Mitchell calls back.

Hawks looks through the back window of the car but sees nothing.

"I can't see him, he's not there!" Hawks shouts.

"He has to be somewhere!" Lockhart looks backwards out of her side window. Nothing.

Mitchell looks out of his side window and there is the familiar profile of a Ford Town Car.

"Shit, he's beside us!"

Lockhart and Hawks spin to look out. Hawks hits the back of Mitchell's headrest in panic as he sees a shotgun barrel pointing out of the window.

"Get down!"

Mitchell pulls Lockhart over towards him as he falls across her. The Russian fires two blasts from his shotgun, hitting the reinforced bodywork of the patrol car. Mitchell slams on the brakes, allowing the Ford to pass them. A horn blasts as an early morning delivery truck swerves to miss the braking car.

"Where the hell are we?" Mitchell asks, as Lockhart looks out of the window.

"Connecticut Avenue, near the Zoological Park, I think."

A tourist sign with an elephant blazon on it flashes past as Mitchell accelerates.

"I have an idea. Al, Daddy's gonna take you to the zoo."

Mitchell changes lane, takes the off ramp, leaving the Ford behind, and heads to the zoo. The police car screeches into the huge car park of the National Zoological Park. There are only a few cars in it at this time of the day, mainly night security and animal welfare vehicles. The police car will stand out and get noticed. Mitchell casts around for somewhere to hide. He sees the main refuse collection bin. Mitchell drives as fast as he can to the larger dumpster. The refuse bin is the size of a truck's trailer. It's huge and set far enough away from any obstruction to allow the collection vehicle to back up, drop off an empty bin and pick up the full one. The police car can easily be concealed behind it and with any luck – and they sure could use some, Mitchell thinks – the car won't be discovered until garbage day. The car is hidden from view and Mitchell switches off the engine. Silence fills the air.

"Now what?" Hawks asks.

Mitchell looks at his watch. It is early, very early in the morning.

"We leave the car here and wait for the first city bus to arrive and ride it back into town."

"Where then?" Lockhart asks.

Mitchell is quiet for what, to the others, seemed like minutes.

"Al's apartment."

* * *

Hawks turns and walks confidently towards his apartment.

"I don't care what time it is, I need a beer and some pizza, and I want it now."

Hawks opens his door and walks in. Mitchell and Lockhart watch Hawks enter the apartment. Both are poised ready for anything, but Hawks seems undisturbed. Perhaps it's too quiet. Mitchell takes the officer's gun out of his holster and is comforted by its weight in his hand. Walking with his back flat against the corridor wall, Mitchell inches towards the open doorway. Lockhart follows, nervously looking at the stairwell they have just come from. Suddenly, Hawks appears at his door.

"You like anchovies?" He has a hands-free phone around his neck. "Well, I do. Screw it, pick 'em off your slice if you don't."

Hawks disappears back inside his room. They follow him in, and Lockhart locks the door behind her. Leaning against it, she drops her shoulders and breathes deeply.

"Pizza is on the way!" Hawks claps his hands together. "I have beer too," Hawks adds. Hawks walks to the kitchen area. "You want one, Mitch?" Hawks asks.

"Not just now, Al, thanks."

The night's events have drawn them closer, and Mitchell welcomes the informality from Hawks.

"Where is your other phone?" Mitchell asks.

"On the table, over there."

Mitchell picks it up and dials.

"Hello?" Hal Cameron's voice was sweet music to Mitchell's ears.

"Hal, it's Paul."

"Jesus, Paul! Where the hell are you? I've been trying to get hold of you all night!" Cameron was sounding like an overanxious parent on prom night.

"It's been a long night, Hal, I'll tell you all about it later. How goes it with you?"

"Good. I've got some new leads for you."

"That's great. Listen, I also need those files you've got. I had best not come into the office, meet me at our usual lunch place. Say, at twelve noon. I'll explain it all then, and you can fill me in then."

"Sure. See you there at high noon."

Mitchell hangs up and turns to Hawks and Lockhart.

"I'll have that beer now."

Hawks throws him a bottle of ice-cold Coors beer. Mitchell twists the top off and takes a long cool drink.

* * *

The buzz from the two beers he has had is wearing off. It is time to go. Mitchell picks up his coat from the floor and moves towards the front door to leave.

"You off, boss?" Hawks asks.

"Going to meet up with Hal Cameron. Listen, Al, I want you to use your skills in finding out as much as you can about the real Rachel Simmons and find out what you can about Karl Hunter too."

"What about Julia, she might be able to help?" Hawks says with trepidation.

Mitchell looks across at the sleeping CIA agent, curled up in an armchair looking like a small vulnerable child, just as she did when she was posing as Simmons.

"Let her sleep for now. I doubt she knows much more than us."

Mitchell opens the door and checks the corridor. Turning back, he sees Hawks looking nervously at the sleeping Lockhart.

"Al, are you okay?"

"Er, you going to leave her. I mean, her and me, alone?"

"Try the NSA computers first, Al. I should be back in an hour or so. Lock the door after me."

"What about me?" Lockhart sits up in her chair, startling Hawks, who jumps.

"You stay here, keep the boy wonder company."

"She's staying here, with me, alone?" Hawks is flushed in the face.

"Is that a problem?" Mitchell asks, knowing his question is going to be awkward.

Hawks looks at Lockhart as if the woman sitting in his armchair, wearing one of his old George Washington University's 'Colonials' basketball sweatshirts and a pair of white gym socks, is in fact an alien species.

"Well, you know, she's a girl and I'm, well, a boy."

"She won't bite you, Al." Mitchell turns to leave, shaking his head in despair at Hawks' pubescence.

"Yeah, but what if I beg?" Hawks splutters out.

Lockhart sits up straight and tries to look more like a CIA operative.

* * *

Cameron enters the restaurant with the now unlit cigarette hanging out of his mouth. Cameron knows where Mitchell will be sitting and heads straight to the table. He sits, with a controlled flop, at the same time as dropping the files on the table.

"Sorry I'm late. Had to wait for a quiet moment to sneak out."

Cameron slides the documents over the table, looking round the restaurant as he does to make sure no one is taking too much notice of them. He needn't have worried; the NFL round-up is on the TV in the corner.

"Thanks. I wanted to check through them, see if we've missed anything."

"And we don't want them to magically disappear either, do we?"

"That too."

"Well, the way things are at the moment, they're probably safer with you, anyway."

"More visits from our friends?"

"I don't know who they are, but they seem to know an awful lot about us."

"Enough to want me dead?"

Cameron looks scared.

* * *

The flat screen of Hawks' computer terminal lights up his and Julia Lockhart's faces as a data stream scrolled from bottom to top in front of their eyes.

"This is looking impossible." Lockhart shakes her head in despair.

The pencil in Hawks' mouth spins excitedly as his tongue twists and rotates the unfortunate wooden shaft like a Werther's Original toffee.

"The trick is to annoy the system so much it tries to lock you out, and once you have done that…"

As if on a cue, the screen goes dark briefly before flashing back into life with a system message.

NSA
Your Gov. Computer Home Link SYSTEMS ENTRY WARNING
You Are Not Authorized to Access This Page

"Bingo!" Hawks' smile is so broad, the pencil in his mouth drops to his desk. "Now we look for the backdoor key," Hawks continues.

"Backdoor key?"

"Yeah, every system has one, that's common knowledge."

"It is?"

"Sure it is. System designers, like the great Gary Kildall, used them all the time to quickly gain access to complex programmes."

"And I should know who Gary Kildall is?"

"Not really, but you should do. He basically invented the personal computer."

"I thought that was Bill Gates and Steve Wozniak."

"When Kildall turned down an offer from IBM to further his own programme design for PCs back in the early '80s, Gates and the great Woz stepped in. By building on work already done, they came up with their Microsoft disk operating system, better known to you and me as MS-DOS. The majority of the world's computers now use MS-DOS, and Gates and Woz are the richest men in the world for it."

"Wow, I bet Kildall is kicking himself."

"He died in 1994. Joe Public is none the wiser about his contribution."

Lockhart takes a sip of coke from a can by the computer screen. Hawk types on his keyboard. Lockhart breaks the silence first.

"You know, I can't help worrying, watching you do this."

"About what?"

"About what is truly private or secret anymore."

Hawks laughs. "There are no more secrets."

"What do you mean?" Lockhart is very curious.

"Double whammy – that's why."

"Come again?"

"Double whammy. There are two inherent problems with all stored data. Number one: it needs to be uploaded into a system, often by someone who has no previous knowledge of the data. So, one becomes two, no longer private or secret, is it? And number two: the computer programme you are uploading needed to be designed by someone first. Therefore, a third person has knowledge of where and how the data is stored. It's a myth to think computer systems are secure."

Hawks smiles as the computer screen rapidly displays:

WELCOME TO THE NSA SECURITY INFORMATION NETWORK
IF YOU NEED ASSISTANCE, CLICK 'HELP' FROM THE MENU BAR.

"Voila, found the key and used it – we're in."

* * *

"Are you sure you can trust this Lockhart woman?" Hal Cameron is trying hard to keep his voice down. However, he knows the urgency of his question is louder than he wanted it to be.

"All I know is the same people who want me dead, want her dead now too."

"The enemy of my enemy is my friend, is that it?"

"We have to start trusting someone."

"What about Sands?"

Like cold water running over a cavity in his mouth, Mitchell winces with the thought that his boss and close friend may want him dead.

"I don't know about Sands. I really don't."

* * *

The computer screen changes from the default setting to a specific file. Lockhart and Hawks read the data with ever increasing urgency.

PAUL MITCHELL.
FILE TEMPORARILY RELOCATED TO HOMELAND SECURITY OFFICE.

"It seems like we're looking in the wrong place. We'll have to get into the Homeland Security computers," Hawks confirms.

"Will that be a problem?"

"Shouldn't be. Not if they've updated the links, which is standard operational procedure. But at least now we know who the bad guys are."

"But that's central government. That's only one step away from the White House."

"I never doubted it for a moment; the buck always stops there." Hawks returns his attention to the computer screen.

* * *

"What was this new lead you said you had for me?" Mitchell asks, temporarily wiping the thought of Sands being part of the dark side of the force from his mind.

"Peter Jones, the guy at the Bureau of Scientific Records, said he had some new information for you."

"Go on," Mitchell urges Cameron to tell him more.

"He didn't tell me – said he would be sending it to you later in the day."

"Is that all?" Mitchell is disappointed.

"He said it was important," Cameron adds. "Want me to go back to the office and check to see if it came in?"

Mitchell looks long and hard at the files on the table.

"Paul?" Cameron is worried about his friend.

Mitchell raises his eyes from the files in front of him.

"You're not worried about whether or not you can trust me, are you?"

Mitchell looks at him evenly.

* * *

The computer screen changes once again:

SECURE FILE
LEVEL 10 SECURITY CLEARANCES ONLY PAUL MITCHELL.

MITCHELL. PAUL
NSA Special Agent Assigned CDM Project Investigation
Scheduled For Termination
With Extreme Prejudice

"Good Christ!" Hawks exclaims.

"What else does it say?" Lockhart grabs hold of Hawks' shoulder.

Hawks scrolls down the screen:

Cross Reference CDM Black File Link: AlphaGammaDeltaGZ

"Can you access that?" Lockhart asks.

"I'm doing it now."

The screen changes once more:

CDM BLACK FILE:
Homeland Security Directive:
By Order of The President
Immediate Termination of Hostile Agents Sanctioned:
KENSINGTON J. – FILE: AS/0958720 (Closed)
MEDVEDENKO A. – FILE: AS/7942033 (Closed)
MITCHELL P. – FILE: AS/4354819 (Open)
LOCKHART J. FILE: AS/127665 (Open)
HUNTER K. FILE: AS/322574 (Open)
CAMERON H. FILE: AS/452785 (Open)
SIMMONS R. FILE: AS/2153203 (Open)

"Holy crap!" Hawks shouts out.

"Yeah – big time."

* * *

Hal Cameron pulls up the collar on his overcoat and looks back at his friend, Paul Mitchell. Mitchell's head is down, and his shoulders are slumped like the man on the ropes he was. As Cameron opens the door to the outside world, cold air rushes in and valiantly assaults the wall of hot air the restaurant air conditioning system has deployed to protect its customers. The pavement outside has been swept clear of snow, but ice is forming in the wind chill now blasting down the street from the river.

Cameron, like many Washington residents at this time of year, curses the Potomac that winds its way through the city like a serpent. The pedestrian crossing near the restaurant is deserted and Cameron carefully makes his way across the frozen pavement towards it.

"Come on, come on." The chant of the pedestrian waiting at crossings the world over on a cold day echoes forth from his icy breath. The west-bound traffic started to slow and then stop.

"At last," Cameron mutters to himself as he looks up to see the red-palmed hand of the stop sign change to the little green man walking. The first step is larger than normal for Cameron as he negotiates the grey slush that had accumulated along the curb. He is quietly impressed with his own agility as he continues across the road.

The tray of dishes hits the floor with a cacophony so loud it immediately snaps Mitchell back out of his thoughts and back into the restaurant. As he does, two women, seated at the windows, scream as they look in horror out at the road. Mitchell rises from the table to see what is happening outside. A uniformed soldier rushes from his table to the door, pushing aside another customer who seems in shock.

Mitchell quickly moves to the large windows at the front of the restaurant and looks out. Lying motionless in the road is Hal Cameron, dark red blood oozing slowly from his head and his shattered legs lying at acute angles to his lifeless body.

"I saw it all," a softly spoken woman next to Mitchell explains, "it just drove directly into him – it never stopped; it was if he wanted to hit that poor man."

* * *

Hawks and Lockhart stare intently at the terminal screen, trying to assimilate the information on the screen. Suddenly the screen refreshes:

KENSINGTON J. – FILE: AS/0958720 (Closed)
MEDVEDENKO A. – FILE: AS/7942033 (Closed)
CAMERON H. FILE:AS/452785 (Closed)
MITCHELL P. – FILE: AS/4354819 (Open)
LOCKHART J. FILE: AS/127665 (Open)
HUNTER K. FILE: AS/322574(Open)
SIMMONS R. FILE: AS/2153203 (Open)

"Oh my God, Cameron." Lockhart instinctively puts a hand over her mouth in shock.

"What does it mean – closed?" Hawks' question is obvious, he just couldn't believe it.

"They killed him," Lockhart says weakly, in shock.

As Hawks looks at Lockhart, a single tear drop forms in her right eye and gently rolls down her face, stopping at the edge of her mouth.

"What do we do now?" Hawks is quietly solemn.

Lockhart wipes her eyes and looks back at the screen.

"Well?" There is a slight edge of panic in Hawks' voice.

"It's not there," Lockhart exclaims.

"What isn't?"

"Your name, it's not in the file; they don't know about you."

"Yet," Hawks pessimistically adds.

"But it means you are safe, and I am too while I'm here."

"But what about the others – Mitch and the rest?"

"Is there any other data stored here?" Lockhart asks.

Hawks looks back at the screen and, using his wireless mouse, clicks a book icon at the top of the screen.

"There is a supplementary file."

Hawks accesses it. The screen changes once again. This time all the names in the original file reappear, but with a link.

"Click on Simmons." Lockhart guides Hawks through the onscreen page.

"Okay."

Hawks moves the mouse arrow over the name Simmons and the pointing fingered fist appears. He clicks.

SUPPLEMENTARY FILE:
NAME: WESTCOTT Rachel (Mother's Maiden Name). / NEE SIMMONS
Rachel.
PRESENT ADDRESS: 1802 MAPLEWOOD DRIVE. WASHINGTON, D.C.
TEL: 202 456 3554

"Got her." Lockhart smiles and punches the air.

The telephone rings startlingly for them both. She picks it up.

"Hello?"

At the other end of the phone, Mitchell is visibly shaking with shock.

"Julia, it's Paul." He pauses, then, "It's Hal, he's—"

Lockhart is so keen to bring Mitchell up to speed with their progress, she interrupts.

"We've located Rachel Simmons. She's using her mother's maiden name of Westcott and—"

Hawks reaches out and touches her arm and the sudden realisation of her interruption becomes apparent to her.

"Hal's dead, Julia," Mitchell continues, "they ran him down while he was crossing the street."

"Oh God, I'm sorry, Paul," Lockhart says. "Are you safe?"

"We have to move fast if we are to warn the others."

"Paul, they don't know about Al yet, we should be safe here. Why don't we go just to *The Washington Post* with all this?"

"It's too late for that now; people are dying. It's gone too far."

"But we need help and—"

"If we don't act now, Simmons and the rest will die like Hal!" Mitchell's grief is quickly changing to anger and rage. "What do you have for me?"

"Her address and contact number."

"Okay, give me her address. In the meantime, you try calling her, get Al to reroute your outgoing calls. Her phone is sure to be wired and he has been able to do that since kindergarten. Warn her, don't panic her, just warn her to get somewhere with plenty of people about, a shopping mall, coffee bar, anywhere there are people."

"Got it. Anything else we should do?"

"Yeah, I want you to go to the Bureau of Scientific Records. There's a librarian there called Dr. Jones. He has some important information for me. Tell him I sent you; I'll meet you there as soon as I can. And Julia, take care."

"You too."

Lockhart hangs up then quickly picks up again.

"Read out Simmons' number for me."

"202 456 3554."

"Paul is going to get Simmons out of that house and into a public place. I'm going to see if I can get her on the phone – it's ringing."

No one picks up.

"Come on, Rachel, pick up the damn phone," Lockhart urges.

Rachel Simmons stands over a worktable in her kitchen, a food blender vibrates slightly as the last few carrot sticks are dropped into the blending blades. The liquid inside the clear plastic jug turns orange, and, after a few seconds, she switches it off. A female radio announcer with a smooth sultry voice announces the station ID.

"*This is WGMS Radio, Washington's oldest and best classical radio station continuing our Mozart festival with violin concerto No1."*

Music plays.

Getting the jug off the blender mount has never been easy, a knack Rachel has never mastered, and tonight is to be no exception. A final twist and a pull and the jug comes away from its base, but not without revenge. Carrot juice washes over the rim of the jug and covers the kitchen phone sitting on the counter.

"Oh, nuts!"

Rachel puts the jug down on the counter and grabs hold of some kitchen towel. The phone is soaked in lumpy orange goo.

"Yuk."

Lockhart hangs up.

"Shit. She's either not in or we're too late."

Grabbing her coat from the back of a chair and picking up her handbag, she checks to see if her gun is inside, then swings the bag onto her shoulder and moves to the apartment door.

"Where are you going?" Hawks asks urgently.

"Paul will be there shortly. I'm going over to the Scientific Records Institute; Paul wants me to pick something up. I'll see you back here later."

"Be careful!" Hawks is suddenly left alone with his computer and, for the first time in his life, his computer is not enough company.

Chapter Seven

The drive out to Simmons' home gives Mitchell time to reflect on what has happened. Could Hal be dead? Jesus Christ, he is. Would Sands be devastated too, he wonders? What the hell is going on? Kensington is dead. Was it suicide? Mitchell doesn't think so. Someone knew he was dead and took the letters. Medvedenko too. Julia was a patsy – not the first time the CIA used one of those, he thinks. *But why try and throw me off the trail?* What would he find out if he talks with these people? The need to get to Simmons before someone else does makes his foot press down harder on the accelerator.

Simmons looks back into the kitchen. It once again resembled the kitchen she awoke to this morning; the tabletops are clean and tidy, and the dishes done. She takes her glass of carrot juice and walks out of the kitchen as the lights go out in the kitchen and come on in the hall. Unknown to her, the kitchen backdoor slowly opens.

* * *

A yellow cab pulls up to the steps outside the Bureau and Lockhart steps out into the cold air. It starts snowing heavily.

Lockhart is unaware she is being watched from across the street. The building is closing for the night as she strides up to the reception desk, where the receptionist is packing away for the night.

"Excuse me, I'm looking for Dr. Jones?"

"Dr. Jones? Yes, he should still be here. He's in the library. That's located in the Goddard Hall, on your right."

Lockhart nods. "Thanks."

"But we are about to close!"

"I'll leave with the doctor," Lockhart calls back without turning.

* * *

Rachel Simmons walks from the kitchen, along the short passageway, to the living room. Although she is the only one at home, the house seems busy and alive. This is due to her smart new digital home economy system she had recently installed at great expense, since CDM money is of little importance to her anymore. Wired into the entire house, the system operates an energy-efficient sensor system. Motion sensors are in every living space in the house. The system switches lights on and off and controls the temperature throughout the house, heating in winter and cooling in summer. The bonus is that an entertainment system is also wired into the house using the same technology. Wherever she goes, music or television or streamed films can be played via small, flat plasma screens dotted throughout the house.

The programmable system operates by a handheld remote or by the master control panel situated under the stairs. Her friends told her she was a techno freak. The guys thought it was cool, however, while her girlfriends felt it was all compensating for not having a family of her own. Maybe, she had thought to herself, life immediately after CDM wasn't easy.

She lays out a square exercise mat on the carpet and as she prepares herself for her third and last yoga session of the day, she recalls how it had taken her a considerable amount of time to get her life back so that she could function as a human being. Still the aftermath of working on the CDM project plays out in her mind like a stuck record, repeating the same arguments and flashes of images, faces, places and that night of discovery.

Not long ago, those images would have brought her out into a cold sweat and given her heart palpitations, a sign of her mind ruling her physical body or stress. Many of the images that flash across her mind's eye are still painful and that is why she practises yoga three times a day.

"That, my dear friends, is the real reason I have my house alive with light and music. To drown out my thoughts."

She cannot tell them that, of course, but it helps to remind herself, from time to time, and keeps her in touch with sanity. Each day she faces a battle, a battle for her serenity.

Drink and drugs were the obvious option, but it was never her bag, not even at college where it was considered par for the course. She knew many scientists who had chosen that path, and they were either dead or dying because of it. No, for her, yoga and the chanting of her own specially given mantra are what works better than anything else. Tonight, she is serene in mind and body. At peace with herself and with a quality of life she has strived to acquire since leaving her life behind after CDM.

The music on the radio stops momentarily as the announcer pauses to issue the bottom of the hour weather report. Gracefully, Simmons slides into the lotus position on her soft green mat and listens to the soft warm voice of the radio DJ.

"*The weather forecast for the D.C. area tonight is for heavy snowfalls, with the chance of some lightning. Yes, lightning thrown in for good measure. Records do show, however, that this is not the first time the D.C. area has had lightning and snowstorms, the last such occurrence was way back in 1956. So why not stay nice and close to your radio and let us warm you up with some more hot music from our Mozart collection."*

Music plays. Letting the music drift over her, she slowly closes her eyes and begins the deep rhythmic breathing required to maintain her mantra. As she does, the hall lights come on and a shadow falls across the carpet just outside the living room entrance. A figure, silent and completely still, watches her every move. The lights switch off.

* * *

The large austere library at the Scientific Records Institute appears to be deserted. Only a few of the overhead lights are switched on, which makes the library even more inhospitable. The large, ornate, arch-shaped, stained glass windows that run along the outside wall of the library building momentarily light up in a burst of colour as lightning hidden deep inside the snowstorm outside strikes an unsuspecting part of the city.

Lockhart moves through the aisles of bookcases looking for Dr. Jones.

"Dr. Jones? Are you still here?"

There is no reply.

For the first time, she notices her own footfall, loud and exposing. Nearing the end of the long bookcase, another lighting strike illuminates the open space reading area directly in front of her.

"Are you looking for me?"

Lockhart jumps back startled.

"Oh, I'm terribly sorry, I didn't mean to startle you, but I heard someone calling my name. This thundersnow is quite rare, you know, at sea level anyway. It is a dear diary moment."

Regaining her composure quickly, "Are you Dr. Peter Jones?"

"I am. What can I do for you, er, Miss…?"

"Lockhart, Julia Lockhart."

* * *

Sitting at the computer terminal, Hawks stares intently at the screen.

FILE: AS/786132 CROSS REF:GZ/00000 HUNTER K.
PROFESSOR
FORMER CDM TEAM LEADER.
LOCATION AURORA RESEARCH SHIP – Status: AT SEA

* * *

Unlike the other case files he had looked at, this one was different. The reference number for starters – five zeros. Zeros were not normally used and the single flashing star at the bottom of the data screen indicated the file was currently being updated.

"*Aurora*, now where have I heard that name before," Hawks thinks out loud.

Hawks picks up the phone next to the computer and dials quickly. The phone rings.

"Gail? Hi, it's Al. Listen, you still do volunteer work for Greenpeace? You do, that's great. Listen, I need a favour. Listen, do you know if the *Aurora* is a Greenpeace ship – it is! That's great, I knew I had heard of her. Listen, babe, could you get the crew list for me? I really need to find out if someone is on board. No, they don't owe me money. Thanks, speak soon."

Hawks hangs up the phone and takes a sip of coke from a can. The phone rings a nd Hawks snaps it up.

"Hello? Babe, you star! Read out the names for me."

Hawks listens intently to the names.

"Thanks, Gail, I owe you one." And Hawks hangs up.

Hawks looks back at the screen.

"You lying piece of shit."

He types onto the keyboard:

REQUEST ACCESS TO FILE: GZ/00000

The reply is swift.

PLEASE ENTER PASSWORD

A box appeared for the password entry.

"To hell with that."

Hawk types onto the keypad and the screen reverts to DOS. Like a classical pianist in the throes of the grand finale of a great work, Hawks' fingers feverishly caress the keys of his computer. Like hail hitting corrugated iron, the sound of a hacker programmer echoes through his apartment.

"There you are. Hello, what are you?"

The screen changes:

T:S3 TOP SECRET
THE NOVA COLLECTIVE R1:8

"Holy shit!"

* * *

The final long and slow exhale of breath concludes Rachel Simmons' final mantra chant. Slowly opening her eyes, she smiles warmly and stands in one flowing movement. Crossing her legs once again, she stretches down and touches her toes, arching her back slightly to remove the stiffness of sitting from her muscles. Standing tall and straight, Simmons empties her glass of carrot juice and heads out into the hall.

A gloved hand clamps around her mouth and twists her violently about, dragging her backwards towards the kitchen. Why hadn't the lights come on? The question instinctively rushed through her mind. Why?

Mitchell walks up to the house and, without pausing, pushes the doorbell. The chimes are clearly audible from outside. No reply.

Simmons is held tightly around the mouth and both arms are pinned behind her. The chimes of the front door are heard again. Despite her struggle, her assailant is far too strong to break free. She relaxes and lets her body go limp; the extra weight momentarily throws her attacker off balance. Feeling the sway, she quickly stands bolt upright and, at the same time, stamps down as hard as she can on the bridge of her attacker's foot.

His hand comes free from her mouth, and she screams as loudly as her full lungs allow. She draws in another breath to scream again but all that surfaces is a gargle of blood and oxygen as the point of the knife pierces her neck and punctures her windpipe. She slumps on the carpet.

"Rachel!"

On hearing the scream, Mitchell tries the door handle, but it is locked. Slamming his weight against it does little and the door holds fast. Taking a step back, he draws his gun and fires two shots at the door lock, sending splinters of wood across the porch. Ramming the door with his entire body, it opens.

Mitchell stumbles into the darkness of the hall. He raises

his gun, desperately trying to see what is there in the gloom. His gun is knocked out of his hand by a kick, his wrist joint cracking with the impact. Recoiling from the blow, turning he is slashed across the shoulder by a knife.

"Ah! Jesus!" Mitchell instinctively grabs his shoulder. Blood spurts through his coat.

Looking in the direction of the attack, he can see a man briefly silhouetted against the door opening, as the figure lunges forward again. Blocking the thrust with his left, Mitchell swings a fast right cross, hitting the attacker hard on the side of his face, just below the ear. The momentum of the counter punch and Mitchell's sidestep makes the attacker stumble.

"You fucker!"

Mitchell kicks out as hard as he can, toe pointing into the anus of the attacker. The force of the blow pushes the attacker forward, his head hitting and knocking over a small table. Mitchell gropes blindly in the dark, his hand searching wildly along the carpeted floor for his gun. The attacker clambers up from the floor. Mitchell turns and sees the glint of a steel blade, as his eyes become accustomed to the light. Mitchell's hand closes around the grip of his gun. Quickly and without aiming, he fires blindly into the dark. The cordite flashes illuminate the hall, like a strobe light at a nightclub.

The attacker stumbles backwards, grabs his side in pain, and runs straight at Mitchell, barging him to one side to get through the open doorway. He disappears into the snow-covered street outside. Mitchell runs to the door and aims his gun, but the attacker is gone. A trail of speckled blood guides Mitchell's eyes towards a car being driven away at speed.

* * *

Julia Lockhart and Dr. Peter Jones sit opposite each other at a reading desk in the library. The desk is lit by a single desk lamp. The rest of the library has closed for the night and is in darkness. Lockhart looks uneasily around at her surroundings as she places her handbag on the floor by the table.

"Are you alright? Would you like me to put the main lights on? I can, you know, at the main switchboard," Jones enquires.

"No, I'm fine, honestly. Too much of a vivid imagination, lousy on ghost train rides too."

Jones laughs. Through the ornate stained glass windows, the snowstorm continues unabated outside. Occasionally, the whistle of the wind finding its way into the corridors of the library adds to the overall effect of being encased.

"So, what exactly is this information you have for Agent Mitchell?"

"Yes, well, after speaking with Agent Mitchell I became curious about this CDM project, so I checked all the record libraries here in the Unites States – without much success, I'm afraid. However, I did get some help from a friend of mine in London."

Jones reaches into his briefcase on the floor by his chair and produces an A4 photo and drops it on the table. Lightning from the thundersnow once again lights the room.

"This weather freaks me out," Lockhart exclaims.

"Yes, it's quite unusual," Jones agrees, "adverse weather always makes me feel homesick."

Lockhart smiles.

* * *

Mitchell soon finds the manual override switch for the lights. The bright light hurts his already sore eyes. He slowly opens them fully. He wishes he hadn't. Sprawled in an awkward pose on the floor lies the body of Rachel Simmons. A scarlet moat of blood pools around her legs as the blood oozes from an open wound on her neck.

Mitchell kneels, pulling her blood-soaked hair away from her face. She is deathly white. Closing her eyes with his hand, he lowers his head in despair.

* * *

Hawks rereads the printout in his hand and is startled when the phone beside him rings. He picks it up, his gaze not leaving the sheet of paper in his hand.

"Hello?"

"Al, it's Paul, is Julia there?"

"No, she left a while back to run an errand for you, but listen, Paul, I've found something."

"What is it?"

"I've also found Hunter."

Hawks hears a car door being slammed shut and agitated voices, some giving commands. Hawks stands up, taking the telephone with him to the window.

"I managed to access Hunter's file through Homeland Security. It was under the designation 'GROUND ZERO', you heard of it?"

"No."

"Didn't think you would have. This is scary, Paul. I mean, big time, freaky shit, out there scary."

Hawks reaches the window and looks out. Several police cars are parked up, their lights flashing.

"Oh fuck."

"Al, what's wrong?" Hawks' tone has more than a hint of panic in it, Mitchell guesses correctly. "Al?"

"Err, I've got problems here, Paul."

"Al, what is it?"

Hawks rushes back to his desk.

"I've got to go. I'll try and catch up with you later."

Hawks hangs up; the monotone buzz Mitchell hears confirms that. Hawks pushes a CD into the side slot of his computer and presses Ctrl S. The screen changes:

SAVE TO DISC

A bar starts filling at the bottom of the screen.

"Come on, come on."

The screen changes once again:

WARNING: UNAUTHORIZED ACCESS. FILE ERASER ACTIVATED.

"Oh shit!"

There is a loud banging on the door.

"Alvin Hawks, this is the police. We have a warrant for your arrest. Open this door now!"

Hawks grabs the disc from the computer:

JOB INTERRUPTED

Hawks quickly types a few keys and the screen changes yet again:

HAWKS' VIRUS RELEASED

The images on the computer screen dissolve as if acid had been dropped on to them. The back window opens easily, just as he had practised, and the fire escape is a welcome sight. The loud banging continues at the door, as Hawks scrambles through the window, shutting it behind him. It is cold, much colder than he thought, and in his rush to leave he left his lovely, warm, duck-down filled North Face jacket back in his apartment. But he sure as hell wasn't going back for it now.

The apartment door surrenders to the size twelve Elephant D boot of the officer and flies open. Five men burst into the apartment and quickly establish a search for Hawks.

* * *

"Where exactly in London is this information coming from?" Julia Lockhart examines the image.

"A dear and old friend of mine who works at the British Library. It moved, you know, after the refurbishment. No more the grandeur of the reading rooms in the museum. Now, St Pancras, off the Euston Road, is where you will find the greatest collection of books and manuscripts since the great library of Alexandria."

"Really? I didn't know that."

"Not that he's bitter, of course, but who could blame him? I spoke to him recently. Anyway, he said he'd investigate it for me."

"I don't mean to be rude but, how can someone hundreds of miles away find something we couldn't find here, where it was generated?"

"You see, the British Library receives almost all the world's published scientific journals and some of the original documents too, for the collection. A bit like your National Archives, but since we had no luck here, I figured London must have a record of it somewhere and they did."

"And this photo is in the documents the British Library has?"

"Yes, and some other material too. He is a straight bat type, Charles; he is faxing it over tonight. A decent chap that. I'll tell you what," Jones continues, "why don't you go and wait for it to come through in my office? I have some other work I could be doing, as Captain Oats famously once said. I won't be long, no need for both of us to be out here. There should be some super Indian tea in the caddy. Why not have a brew? I could sure do with a fresh cup."

"Okay, I will, thanks. I'm not sure I can make proper tea though." Lockhart is embarrassed.

"Nothing to it, dear, if you warm the pot first and always, but always, put the milk in the cup before the tea. Stops the china from cracking. Besides, you'll find the whole process very therapeutic," Jones explains.

"I'll do my best." Lockhart stands and smiles warmly. Perhaps some stereotypes are justified. She turns and heads off into the darkness towards the only light she can see, in Jones' office.

Jones' office is as she expects: neat and tastefully decorated. On the wall hang several pictures, mainly school portraits and cricket teams. Jones in front of a Henley boathouse-rowing club and other sporting venues too – Wimbledon, Lord's, which Lockhart had to read the label to identify, and a rugby match at Twickenham.

The kettle boils quickly and, finding the china cups neatly washed and stored on a tea tray on a nearby table, she dutifully warms the pot with hot water from the kettle. While the tea brews, she recalls her grandmother, whose mother was English, telling her that tea needed to brew for a good three minutes. She pours what she hopes will be the right amount of milk into two small china teacups. She admits to herself the tea making process is indeed very therapeutic.

Lockhart moves to the open office door and calls out, "Dr. Jones, the tea is ready. Would you like me to bring it over?"

There is no reply.

"Dr. Jones, the tea is ready!"

Nothing. Then she hears a scuffling sound, followed by a dull thud.

"Now what?"

Lockhart looks for her handbag where her service revolver is tucked away. Like a slap in the face, she realises where she had left it: at the table with Jones. She is unarmed. Lockhart looks back out into the darkness of the library, unfamiliar and menacing. She looks down at her feet and removes her shoes. By her third step, she is well and truly into the darkness.

Feeling one's own heartbeat is a discomforting sensation as it usually means an event is about to take place that will affect your life; your first kiss with a new partner, the immediacy of news, good or bad, or the feeling of fear. Right now, Lockhart's heart is pumping hard with fear. The urge to run for the door is almost overwhelming, but Jones is in here somewhere and he might need help. The office fax machine rings. Lockhart looks back towards the warmly lit office.

"Dr. Jones?"

Lockhart stops at the end of one aisle, peering into the darkness.

"Are you alright?"

The library remains silent. Another discharge of lightning illuminates the library. Halfway down the aisle, books lie scattered on the floor. Lockhart moves cautiously down the aisle ever closer to where she last saw Jones. Lockhart emerges from an intersection, created by two tall rows of bookcases, into the reading area where she and Jones looked at the photo together. The desk lamp is no longer on, and it is difficult to see the desk, let alone her handbag with her gun in it. Peering deep into the darkness, she looks instinctively around for any signs of Jones. Nothing.

Lightning flashes outside once again, momentarily illuminating the library. Standing to Lockhart's right, only inches away from her, where a second ago she was looking into what she thought was nothing but darkness, stands a tall figure dressed in black. Lockhart's scream of surprise catches in her throat. A knife flashes as she turns and runs silently in her stocking feet towards the desk and her gun. The blade slashes her down one side of her arm.

Managing to keep her balance, she scrambles towards the desk and falls to her knees searching for her bag. A hand reaches out for her, catching her by the hair, and stops her abruptly from moving any closer to the desk. Dragged backwards back down the aisle, Lockhart kicks and twists as hard as she can, her hair straining at the roots as the firm grip holds fast.

Training, training. Quickly changing tempo and struggling to her feet, she moves towards her attacker, her hair falling slack as she gets closer. Now she has the space to move, she twists to face her attacker and with a half-clenched fist hits out at the attacker's throat. Bull's-eye! The release is immediate, as the attacker grabs their throat, gasping for air. She can sense the panic of asphyxiation.

Scrambling away, she stumbles on the fallen books she saw earlier, her feet sliding on the up-turned pages. She kicks out with both feet, trying to find grip. The red-hot pain of the knife slashing her back involuntarily jolts her forward and, finding grip once more, like a sprinter off the blocks, she runs as hard as she can towards Jones' office.

Lightning strikes again and Lockhart checks to see the passageway behind her is empty. She looks to the lights of the office, just a few metres away, and runs. Another lightning strike and she glances behind her again. Nothing. Where the hell is he? Turning forwards again, she sees the office door at last!

Wham! She runs smack into something blocking the doorway. The force of the impact empties her lungs of oxygen, and the first part of her scream is silent. The second part is cut short by a hand over her mouth. She looks up with terror to see who it is that is trying to kill her. Mitchell looks down at her with a worried expression on his face. He takes his hand away from her mouth.

"It's me, Paul."

"Paul, someone's out there."

She slumps against him. Mitchell puts an arm around her waist, supporting her. He helps her into Jones' office, putting her on a couch. His hands are smeared with her blood from the wounds on her arm and back.

"I want a gun, give me a God damn gun!" Lockhart is terrified.

"It's okay, take it easy." Mitchell tries to calm her to no avail.

"Give me a fucking gun, right now!"

Mitchell reaches down to his right trouser leg bottom and reveals a snub-nosed .38 pistol in an ankle holster.

"Here, have this."

He hands her the pistol. She grabs it and holds it tightly, pointing the barrel at the door. Mitchell hits the light switch, plunging them both into darkness.

Mitchell whispers, "Did he have a gun?"

"Not that I saw, just a knife, that was enough for me."

Mitchell draws his gun.

"I think he just killed Simmons."

"Jesus, Paul. Who are these people?"

"I don't know but I aim to find out. He's probably still out there. Are you going to be alright here?"

Lockhart touches Mitchell's shoulder and squeezes it. "I'll be fine but come back."

“I won’t be long.”

“That’s what Captain Oats said.”

Mitchell double takes at Lockhart’s historical reference.

Thankfully the streetlight coming through the stained glass windows high on the front façade of the library casts only a pearly white glimmer as far as the top of the bookcases. The corridors of the bookcases themselves remain in shadow. A level playing field, Mitchell thinks, no advantage to either side, so a fair chance at least.

Leaving the office, Mitchell quickly clears the open space between the office door and the first dark avenue of bookcases. Another lightning flash illuminates the long aisles he has just entered. Once again, the reassuring weight of his service revolver points the way ahead. The sound of distant thundersnow echoes around the library. The passageway, despite the darkness, feels familiar. The books Julia had stumbled over moments ago are on the floor beneath his feet. Stepping over them, he moves quickly to the first intersection, the start of a new length of bookcases.

The muscles surrounding his eyes stretch wide, lifting his eyelids high into his brow to allow in what little light there is. Turning his head left then right, he cannot define anything other than bookcases. He cannot believe the library where he first met Jones is this vast a warren. Moving forward quickly, he stumbles.

“Jesus!”

Reaching out, Mitchell steadies himself against a bookcase. The shock reflex of calling out has revealed his position. Mitchell stands still and holds his breath. His ears twitch, like radar searching in all directions for the sound of movement. Lightning flashes blaze light for a fraction of a second across the library and Mitchell looks down to see what he stumbled over. The head of Peter Jones stares coldly back at him, frozen in a death mask of shock and pain. Surrounding Jones is a pool of blood. Like Simmons, his throat has been cut, as if he were a sacrificial lamb.

Mitchell leaps to his feet and stands, shocked. Taking a few steps back away from the body, his feet slide on the blood. Mitchell reverses into a bookcase, which stops his retreat. He takes a deep breath and investigates the darkness. Lighting once again lights the room. Without warning, a hand bursts through a row of books behind him. Then another bursts through, this one with a knife, thrusting out, just missing his ear and swinging back in an arc towards his face.

Mitchell ducks the blade, narrowly missing the top of his head. Spinning away from the bookcase, pitching backwards, and crashing up against the opposite side, Mitchell opens fire at the retreating hand. Bullets rip into the books, as he empties the gun. The attacker's knife clatters to the floor and the gun clicks as the hammer strikes an empty chamber. The bookcase topples forwards and Mitchell raises his arms in defence as the huge rack of books crashes down on top of him. Silence fills the library once again, as the figure of a man looms over the wreckage of the bookcase.

Lockhart lies uncomfortably on the couch as the pain from her cuts causes her to drift in and out of consciousness. The sound of footsteps approaching the office brings her around and more alert. Raising her gun to point it at the doorway, she supports the gun's weight on her knee. The footsteps grow closer, then stop.

Weakly she calls out, "Paul, is that you?"

The library remains silent. Forcing herself up off the couch, she staggers to the doorway, peering out into the inky blackness. From behind her, the fax machine bursts into life again. Startled, she turns, pointing the gun at the unexpected noise.

At that moment, a black shape darts into the office, smashing into her. She is slammed to the ground. The gun is knocked from her hand and slides out of reach. She looks up with the last pulse of energy she has left before fainting unconscious. The lights of the office come on. The fax machine in the corner begins to spew out paper.

A picture emerges on the fax paper. The picture is titled by hand, *The CDM Team – hope it helps*. The transmission ends. Pulling the picture from the machine, the assassin folds the image and puts it in his pocket.

Books lie scattered on the floor; Mitchell emerges from beneath them. Taking a moment to clear his head, he quickly reloads his gun and jogs to Dr. Jones' office. To Mitchell's right, he hears the sound of a door slamming.

Pausing to listen, there is nothing more. The library falls quiet again. Mitchell continues and enters the dark office. It seems as he had left it. Putting the light on, he sees Lockhart on the floor, just in front of him. He rushes to her, lifting her head, carefully. She opens her eyes, smiling weakly.

"Julia, don't worry. I'll get you out of here."

Mitchell starts to lift her.

"No." She winces in pain. "No, the cuts are deep, and I couldn't stop the bleeding. Please don't move me. It feels like I'm on fire."

"I'll call an ambulance."

Mitchell goes over to Jones' desk and picks up the telephone and dials 911.

"This is Paul Mitchell of the NSA. I need an ambulance at the Scientific Records Bureau, immediately, code blue. Someone's been badly hurt." He pauses for a moment while the operator confirms details. "Right, okay."

Mitchell hangs up the phone, returning to kneel beside Lockhart.

"They're on their way."

Mitchell takes off his jacket, placing it under her head.

"It's going to take them time to get through the traffic in this weather, can I at least lift you up onto the couch?"

"No, I'll be fine here."

"Jones is dead."

Lockhart closes her eyes.

"Did he tell you what he had found out?"

"No. It was all in a fax coming from London. It seems the bastard who got me, got the fax too."

From behind Mitchell, the fax machine, once again, comes to life.

"Now what?" Mitchell asks.

"More from London?"

"I'll look."

Mitchell stands by the fax and a sheet of paper comes out. Printed on it reads:

ERROR PRINT CODE. FX001 RE-TRANSMITTING MESSAGE.

Mitchell takes the paper off the machine and reads it. The fax begins to print again. The picture of the CDM team re-emerges. Mitchell picks it up and looks at the image. Kensington, Medvedenko, Simmons, Hunter are all there. So is Simon Lawrence, from the Science Grant Allocations Unit, but here, in the picture, he is identified as General David Hughes, Military Intelligence and Head of Project Security.

"Hughes, General David Hughes, is the 'es' from Kensington's letter. A presidential appointment; he's the Joint Chief of Staff, for fuck's sake!"

From the library outside, the sound of a door slamming is heard. Footsteps approach as lights in the library slowly flicker on.

Mitchell rushes to switch off the office lights again. It is too quick to be the ambulance, he reasons. Moving over to

Lockhart, he motions her to remain quiet. Mitchell stands to the side of the doorway, his body flat against the wall. The footsteps get closer. A figure enters the doorway. Mitchell pushes his gun against the person's head, hitting the light switch at the same time. A frightened Al Hawks stands ridged.

"It's me! It's me!"

"You scared the piss out of me!" Mitchell lowers the gun.

"Out of you?" Hawks replies sarcastically, looking down at his damp sneakers. "You know you could give someone a heart attack pulling a gun like that." Hawks notices Lockhart lying on the floor. "What the hell happened? Are you okay?"

Hawks walks over to Lockhart and kneels beside her.

"It's Lawrence. The guy I met at the Grant Allocations Unit. Look." Mitchell shows Hawks the fax photograph. "He was in the CDM team as Head of Project Security. Of course, he was using his real name then, General David Hughes."

"You mean President Andrews' personal enforcer? The big daddy of all the neo-cons on the Hill."

"The one and the same. That was the information Jones had for me."

"Well, it makes sense now with what I have. Where is Jones, by the way?"

Mitchell looks out into the now bright library. "Dead. Hughes killed him. He'll be going after Hunter now."

Hawks looks up at Mitchell. "I wouldn't be so sure about that. While I was surfing the Homeland Security files, I stumbled onto a clandestine site for something called the 'Nova Collective'. A secret cabal of scientists and government. They seem to be a neo-con organisation. Twelve members all appointed by President Andrews."

"Shit, I didn't know that." Mitchell is stunned that a cabal the NSA didn't know about existed.

Hawks continues, "I had to dive deep – I mean, really deep

– to find out what I could. Anyway, the Ground Zero file is imbedded in a file in the 'Nova Collective' pages under the code name R1:8. It was buried so deep in a security web that it was impossible not to trigger alarms when I accessed it. Once the security system was triggered, the file automatically erased and transmitted a Leonardo-type virus down the modem link to wipe out the intruding computer."

Lockhart twinges with pain as Hawks holds her injured shoulder warmly.

"I managed to get most of it downloaded onto disc before I released my counter measures."

"Counter measures?"

"Sure, it's a digital war out there. It stops a computer from source tracking my network. It also creates a firewall round my hard drive."

"Silly question." Mitchell is none the wiser.

Hawks takes out a computer disc from his jacket pocket.

"I didn't have time to get it all though, but what I did managed to read of it makes me wonder if we should just get the hell out of this, now."

"What the fuck are you talking about, Al?"

Hawks looks back to the semi-conscious form of Lockhart, then back to Mitchell.

"As far as I can make out, all these people you have been looking for – Hunter, Simmons, the entire CDM network, Medvedenko included – were all under the protection of the Nova Collective when they left CDM. It has been the Nova Collective who have been running your investigation, not you. They have been sending you down rabbit holes from day one. But they just didn't allow for your tenacious, investigative savvy. Their covering up was, at least in your eyes, shabby. They left more clues than they wanted to."

"Covering what up?" Mitchell is frustrated.

"All I know, it happened right about the time CDM shut down and it was something massive. So massive the entire top echelon of the US Government shut it down and sat on it by creating the Nova Collective."

"Sat on what?" Mitchell is getting ratty. It could have been the pain he was still in, of course.

"You tell me! You're the intel spook here not me." Hawks throws Mitchell the disk. "If you don't believe me, check it out for yourself. It's not much but it's enough for me to know we should just get out while we're still able to."

Lockhart moans, opening her eyes. Hawks looks down at her.

"How are you doing, honey?"

Lockhart looks up and sees Hawks' face looking down at her.

"I've been better. It was a hell of a fight you should see the other guy."

"It looks like he won."

"Thanks."

Mitchell walks over to them. "What about Hunter?"

"Yeah, I called a friend at Greenpeace on that – Hunter isn't on the *Aurora* or any of their research ships for that matter."

"Where is he then? Is his location on this disc? Can you access it from Jones' computer here?"

"Sure, but you don't need to. He's working at the Clarke Observatory. I remembered that bit. See what I mean? There is only one reason to falsify a government record – a cover-up."

"Okay, Al, you've convinced me. You stay with Julia; the ambulance is on the way."

"Where are you going? Aren't you going to read that file first?"

"No, I just want Hughes. If he's after Hunter, then that's where I'm going. It's over for you two. When the cops come, mention my name and Sands. She'll look after you now."

Mitchell pauses at the door and looks at Julia on the floor.

"Don't worry, I'll take good care of her," Hawks reassures him. "Good luck, man."

"Don't let me down, Al. Take good care of yourself too." Mitchell turns and leaves.

Chapter Eight

Mitchell's car races up Arthur C. Clarke Observatory Road, along a snowy mountain track that is bordered on one side by the mountain and on the other by a barbed wire fence that has seen better days. The track is rutted and worn. The heavy work vehicles that once dragged the component parts of the observatory up the three-mile winding road to the summit for assembly had left their mark like a signature in wet concrete. The higher Mitchell drives, the clearer the sky becomes, until the snow clouds break, and the night sky fills the heavens like a heavy veil. Bright stars on a dark-blue backdrop lie across the top of the mountain like a curtain. Mitchell's car pulls up outside the observatory's main entrance.

The rare air is even colder than at sea level. It is also noticeably thinner too and it requires three or four breaths before he finds the rhythm he needs to breathe and walk without gasping. The observatory, from the outside, appears quiet, and a dull, blue ceiling-mounted security light shines from inside the glass-fronted lobby. Drawing his gun, he enters the unlocked building.

The telescope is impressive in size. A vitriolic brass plaque by the entrance doors states that the Clarke Telescope is the largest of its type in the United States, beating the University of Chicago's Yerkes telescope by two inches. Mitchell smiles to himself. *Jesus, penis envy, maybe, but telescope envy?*

The interior of the domed area seems deserted. Soft, ground-level lightning illuminates the huge optical telescope from below, casting shadows on the curved walls that provoke memories of Fritz Lang's masterpiece *Metropolis*. An open-plan office suite containing computers and electronic instruments, none of which Mitchell recognises, occupies a space opposite the main doors. The entire area under the semi-sphere seems deserted. Mitchell wonders if Al got it all wrong.

Unannounced, the giant dome above his head shudders to life. A loud grinding of gears, metal on metal, fills the air as the huge dome opens and the black sky appears through the crack. The lights in the observatory switch to red as the opening in the roof stops at fourteen metres.

"Hello there. I hope I didn't startle you."

Mitchell turns, looking for the source of the voice. Standing high up on a gantry encircling the interior of the dome stands a man.

"I'll be down with you in a moment."

Mitchell studies the man coming down the metal gantry steps. The photograph of Hunter he had seen showed a much younger, virile-looking man, with Hollywood good looks. Could this be the same man? All Mitchell had read about Hunter pointed to a man on the cusp of breaking into the elite of the world's most renowned scientists with the good looks of Robert Redford that would make television networks around the world clammer for him to present science documentaries. If he were for sale, he could get $50 million from any network or government. The man before him now was not what he was expecting.

A shadow of his former self is a kind reflection. Hunter's hair is thin, wispy and receding, and his frame is weak.

Muscles that were once firm and defined are now soft. As he approaches, Mitchell can see his eyes are sunken and dark. His general pallor is ashen, and a silver crucifix hangs around his neck. Odd for a man of science, Mitchell thought. What the hell had happened to him?

"I'm afraid it takes me a little while longer to do this than it used to."

Mitchell holsters his gun. "I'm Paul Mitchell, NSA."

Mitchell extends his hand and Hunter accepts it warmly. Mitchell can feel the bones of his hand as they shake.

"I know who you are, Agent Mitchell. I have been expecting you."

"You have?"

"Oh yes. And, of course, you know who I am?"

"Professor Hunter, I assume."

Hunter laughs. "Like Stanley and Livingstone at Lake Tanganyika, we finally meet. You have indeed brought me new life."

"Professor, we believe your life is in danger."

Hunter moves away. Mitchell watches as Hunter walks slowly towards what looks like a leather reclinable armchair, situated at the eyepiece of the telescope.

"Oh, I don't think so, Agent Mitchell." Hunter slumps into the chair with a deep sigh. "You see, I know all about you and your investigation into the deaths of my dear friends." Hunter pauses and looks lost in deep thought for a moment, then continues. "You see, I know everything."

Mitchell joins Hunter at the telescope.

"You deserve an explanation, Agent Mitchell. Please sit, there should be a chair or stool in the office somewhere."

Mitchell sees a science lab stool nearby and pulls it over and sits near Hunter.

"Six years ago, I was heading the last of the CDM night

shifts at Goddard. The hunt for Cold Dark Matter was the cutting edge of my type of astronomy. Joining the CDM Team was a great opportunity for me. John, Anton, and Rachel were the tops in their field. But on that night, it all ended."

"Just because the funding stopped?" Mitchell asks.

Hunter huffs. "You still have no idea what this is all about. I suppose that confirms my methods were sound."

"I don't understand."

"You will. Tonight, it must all end and you will end it for me. I've had enough."

Hunter's eyes have the look of what clinical psychologists call the 1,000-yard stare. The unfocused gaze of people experiencing acute stress or suffering from a traumatic recent event.

Hunter continues, "Death is a blessed relief from the burden of knowledge, Agent Mitchell."

"What knowledge? What burden? What happened to you? You look—" Mitchell is interrupted.

"Old?" Hunter laughs. "Do I really?" Hunter feels his face and looks at his hands. "I suppose I do. They said when Moses came down from Mount Sinai, after speaking with God, he too had aged."

"Are you saying you have spoken with God?"

Thoughtfully, Hunter replies, "Perhaps I have."

Mitchell is lost for words. Hunter looks up past Mitchell and behind him.

"You have met General Hughes, of course."

Mitchell turns sharply only to be struck hard across the face with a gun. Mitchell falls to the floor.

"Enough of this!" Hunter shouts angrily. "Put that gun away and help him up."

Hughes reluctantly puts the gun into his jacket pocket and lifts Mitchell back up onto his seat. Hughes reaches into

Mitchell's pocket and takes his gun. As soon as Hughes reaches in and takes his gun, Mitchell realises he gave his back up weapon to Julia, back at the library.

"I'm sorry. Are you alright?" Hunter asks.

Mitchell has a large bruise on his cheekbone to add to his collection.

"I'll live. An addition to my others, courtesy of Hughes and his henchmen."

Hunter's 1,000-yard stare is not showing any sign of empathy to Mitchell's plight. Then Hunter continues.

"When our Cold Dark Matter discovery was brought to the attention of the White House, Hughes was assigned to oversee the security of the entire project. The data, the people who collected it, the technicians and us the scientists."

"What discovery?"

"Patience, Agent Mitchell, your journey is near its end." Hunter taps the eyepiece of the telescope. "When we searched the heavens for Cold Dark Matter, we used a technique called Gravity Wave detection. Large objects, visible or not, regardless of hot or cold temperature, leave a wake. Not unlike that of a ship at sea, as objects move in space, they leave a wake. These waves are an indicator of mass. The missing mass in the universe."

"Go on." So far so good; Mitchell was keeping up.

"Messier 101, Agent Mitchell, a spiral galaxy first discovered in 1781, is a system well known to us astronomers. John had found some gravity wave fluctuations there. I went back to calibrate an experiment and found what we thought was a supernova explosion in the outer spiral, a massive event, even in space terms, ripping apart a huge portion of the galaxy in the process. We were excited, very excited! What a way to go out, with a galaxy-busting bang! But there was something odd about Supernova 101. The data was not what we had expected. Even after CDM was shut down, John, Anton, Rachel, and I worked on the data. For months we couldn't work out what was wrong, then Anton noticed that the gravity wave structure, what we were geared up to look at in the first place, was where the solution lay. The loss of energy where the gravity wave frequencies decreased didn't tally with the spectral data we had got. In places, peaks were observed where energy levels were low. It was as if a light was being switched on and off between the two data streams. It then dawned on us that this was not natural in origin – it was created. In other words, artificial."

"You mean, made by aliens?" Mitchell was incredulous.

"At first, we thought like you. We checked all the data again, any possible sources of corruption from Earth, everything, but the conclusions were emphatic."

"So what was it?"

"A message, Agent Mitchell, or to be more precise, a warning, written in a simply binary code that was easy to break. We were meant to read it."

"You mean it was directed at us?"

"Oh. Most definitely."

"By whom?"

"We don't know their name, Agent Mitchell."

"Okay. What did the message say?"

Hunter sits back further in the leather chair, subdued and broken. He looks like a helpless, defeated, lost soul, and yet, in a voice that was powerful and ominous, he replies, "Agent Mitchell, beside you, is a computer. Open the screen and press enter. It's all set up for you. Please."

Mitchell looks over at a small desk with a laptop. Mitchell slides over to the desk, opens the screen and presses enter. The screen immediately comes to life.

"What you are about to see is the decoded message. We

know it was meant for us, as the point of origin in the message was Sol 3. Earth, Agent Mitchell."

An animation of the solar system appears – it reminds Mitchell of the 1970s NASA animation for the old Voyager missions. Soon, the giant planets flash past, and then the outer planets, until the animation screen is a huge star field.

"What the hell is this?"

Hunter is silent.

Mitchell is transfixed by the stars and galaxies appearing on the screen.

"Is this still animation or for real?" Mitchell asks.

Again, silence from Hunter.

The colours are mesmerising. Like the deep space Hubble or James Webb images of the universe, they were humbling. Then, as suddenly as the images started, they stop, or seem to. Minutes go by, and then, ever so slowly, an image begins to take form on the screen.

"What is that?" Mitchell asks.

Hunter just smiles softly as the image on the screen gets clearer and clearer. The image clarifies and Mitchell slowly realises he is looking at an object, not of natural construction.

"Shit! Is that what I think it is?!"

The scale of the object is colossal. The 'telescope' image magnifies even further. Mitchell starts to see more and more detail.

"Wait a God damn minute. Is that, I mean, are there people in that thing?"

More detail.

"Holy crap, they're not human. Jesus Christ, what the – aliens? That's impossible. We don't have the technology to see that detail."

"You're correct," Hunter interjects, "*we* don't."

The image from the telescope speeds up and turns to reveal a large, windowed deck area. The size is unimaginably huge. Creatures, bipedal and others with more limbs, are what Mitchell can only surmise as being herded towards a vast empty box.

"Hunter, what is this? Is this a movie hoax or what?"

Mitchell watches as the screen shows a huge door closing on the occupants of the box. After a short while the door opens, and the box is once again empty.

"What happened to those things? What happens inside that box?"

Hunter looks coldly at Mitchell and, in a matter-of-fact voice, says, "We concluded, after years of watching the images, that it is some sort of factory ship. Like the fish processing ships of the deep ocean, they catch and process organic life on one ship. Those poor creatures, like the fish in our oceans, Agent Mitchell, are being processed."

"You mean this film is from the decoded data of the Nova explosion?"

"Yes, and there is something else." Hunter slowly gets up from his chair and stands as straight as he can. "Within the message, there was a subatomic signature, carbon-14. Now, carbon-14 exists in all living things on Earth. I mean everything: trees, animals, people, everything that is living, and these atoms are always decaying, but in turn they are being replaced by new carbon-14 atoms at a constant rate through cosmic rays."

"Carbon dating." Mitchell knows the theory.

"That's right. That is how we can tell how old anything is, by the amount of decay within the carbon-14. And in the message, we found a carbon-14 signature."

"But all life near the explosion would have been wiped out."

"It would most certainly have killed all life anywhere near it," Hunter affirms.

"But you see, Agent Mitchell, the decay we measured was not finite, it was constant."

"Constant?" Mitchell is stunned.

"This was an ancient civilization. It must have been to have the technology to encode a message, in that cataclysmic moment of destruction, to warn us. It is reasonable to assume that they were powerless to stop it from happening to them. Agent Mitchell, the carbon-14 decay is a countdown clock, a countdown to Ground Zero – us."

"Jesus," Mitchell exclaims.

"Indeed. All of us who worked on the CDM team – John, Anton, Rachel, and I – all knew the date of reckoning to the precise hour. But we all swore never to reveal it."

"Why?"

"Think about it," says Hughes, "the proof is undeniable and once word got out, there would be anarchy, panic, and mayhem. Mr. Hughes was assigned to make sure none of us – John, Anton, Rachel or I – would ever speak of the day to come."

Hunter walks slowly to the small office. Mitchell, under the watchful eye of Hughes, follows.

"We made a suicide pact, Agent Mitchell, if the burden became too great, we would end it by our own hand and if we couldn't actually kill ourselves, well, Mr. Hughes here is more than qualified to see that the job got done."

Hunter enters the office suite and Mitchell follows.

"Like I said, you deserved an explanation, but it must end here."

Mitchell feels a gun at his back. Hunter slowly turns to face him.

"Your silence is all that we require, and we must all remain silent for a little while longer."

Mitchell's ears prick up at the sound of a gun being cocked.

"Wait a minute. Why not share this with other scientists like yourself and see what they have to say first. There may be another explanation?"

"You have only just learnt the truth; I have lived with this knowledge for some time now. Don't you think we have looked at everything? Hughes being here, doesn't that tell you anything?"

With a sudden realisation, he understands. The president knows.

Leaping forward, Mitchell grabs Hunter and throws him back across the suite at Hughes. Like a cheap rag doll, the professor crashes against Hughes, sending them both backwards. A shot rings out from Hughes' gun.

Mitchell jumps over a desk, landing awkwardly as he does so. Scrambling to his feet, he runs to the exit.

"Where is he?" Hughes shouts.

Mitchell hits the doors, but they are locked.

"Shit."

Mitchell looks about him. The metal steps leading to the gantry. The old metal frame clangs as Mitchell mounts the first rung.

"He's climbing the gantry," Hunter replies.

"Switch on the day lights," Hughes instructs Hunter as they both get to their feet.

Hunter reaches out to a control panel in the suite and hits four lever switches. The dome suddenly brightens. Hughes looks up to see Mitchell near the top of the dome, on the maze of walkways surrounding the upper level.

Hughes raises his gun and fires several shots. Lying flat on the walkway, the bullets ricochet off the metal structure.

"I'm going up after him."

Mitchell gets up and starts to climb onto the next level walkway, the one he hoped would take him to the telescope opening and outside.

"Close the God damn roof!" Hughes bellows.

Hunter sits at the control desk and types in the instruction. Once again, the gears grind and the metal shutters above Mitchell's head begin to close.

Hughes looks back up through the metal work, but Mitchell can't be seen. He starts to climb. Hughes reaches the top of the ladder, and stepping out onto the gantry, he looks around the circular walkway. Mitchell is nowhere to be seen.

"Where are you, Mitchell?"

"There is no escape," Hughes shouts over the noise of the closing doors.

The air is cold near the top of the roof and Hughes can see his breath. A support frame for the telescope, mounted on wheels that sit in a grooved rail, blocks Hughes' progress. Quickly looking behind over the edge of the support, Hughes makes sure Mitchell isn't hiding behind it. He passes underneath the support and the weight of the mighty telescope and continues along the gantry.

A few feet away, Mitchell holds onto the outside shell of the dome, peering down into the observatory car park below. Mitchell sighs. Shit out of luck again. There was nothing for him to grab hold of, to climb down and to jump would be suicide. The irony is just too much. Nothing for it, he will have to get back inside and out of the door. Pulling himself up, fingers swollen with the effort, he rests his chest on the guide rail of the shutters. The shutters are now only three feet away, so he has to move fast.

Hughes suddenly reappears from behind the support frame. *At last, fortune smiles on me*, Mitchell thinks. In one motion, he swings his legs over the rim and lands directly on top of Hughes. Both men crash to the metal work. Hughes' gun clatters across the gantry. Mitchell manages to pull himself up first and scrambles forward for the gun. Hughes grabs Mitchell's leg. Twisting, Mitchell yells out in pain, as his knee joint is dislocated. Swinging his arm round, he lands a blow to Hughes' head. Reaching out for the gun, his fingers, swollen with blood, claw the pistol grip towards his hand.

"Got it!"

Mitchell turns as Hughes gets to his feet and reaches into his jacket pocket, drawing a long-bladed knife.

"Either I kill you now, or you get processed later. Which will it be?"

Hughes advances towards Mitchell. Without hesitation, Mitchell fires three bullets into his chest. Hughes plummets to the ground. His screams are cut short by the impact. Mitchell stares down at the body of Hughes, lying sprawled on the observatory floor.

The last few rungs of the metal ladder are the worst. Now he is on the ground, he can at least manage the pain of his knee by taking measured steps.

"Don't move."

Mitchell points his gun at Hunter, who is still sitting at his desk with his back to him.

"Turn around, slowly. Hughes is dead. You're the only one left to answer for all of this."

Hunter swivels slowly about on his chair. There is a gun in his hand. He fires. The single shot hits Mitchell in the right shoulder. An involuntary reflex spasm pulls the trigger on his gun, hitting Hunter in the thigh.

Mitchell drops to the floor. Sitting up, he looks at the blood pouring from his shoulder. Taking a handkerchief from his pocket, he stuffs it in the hole. Hunter stumbles out of the suite. Leaning against a desk, he looks down at Mitchell. Mitchell's gun is by his side.

"Don't do it, Agent Mitchell. Be still." Hunter sits on the edge of the desk. "I'm sorry if you're uncomfortable. But you won't be for long."

Mitchell winces with pain as he moves his arm up to rest on his lap.

"Why?"

"With everything I have told you, despite the evidence I have presented to you and yet, you ask why?"

"The alien civilization may not have been able to stop what was going to happen to them, but what makes you so God damn sure we are like them?" Mitchell offers, through clenched teeth.

"Naivety is not a privilege I can enjoy, Agent Mitchell. I know what we as a species are capable of. The good, the bad and the ugliness of twentieth-century history alone tells us that we never learn from our past mistakes. We are a young organic species in a cold dark universe. Nothing more than fish in a cosmic ocean."

Hunter shifts his weight to ease the pain in his leg.

"The proof of our discovery is stored in this computer." Hunter points to the laptop Mitchell used earlier. "You have looked inside Pandora's box, Agent Mitchell; it can never be closed to you."

Mitchell now understands what he means by the burden of knowledge.

"This building is wired to explode; the countdown has already begun. I leave it up to you. You can tell the world if you want to. Many won't believe you at first, or you can let the world have one more night's peaceful sleep. I can no longer bear the burden of that knowledge." Hunter raises the gun to his head. "The choice is yours, Agent Mitchell."

"*No!*"

Mitchell twitches with shock as the gun fires. Hunter's body slumps to the floor. Mitchell struggles to his feet. Looking over to the laptop computer, he can see a black box with digital numerals counting down.

Mitchell hobbles over to the timer. A single key control arms or disarms the mechanism.

12… 11… 10… 9… 8…

Mitchell raises his hand and reaches out towards the key. Images of the people most important to him in his life flash across his mind's eye…